The baby's crib was empty!

Megan hurried down the stairs, then went still, her breath catching in her throat.

Stretched out on the sofa as much as his long legs would allow, Jake lay with baby Matthew, who was sound asleep, cradled securely against his chest.

The sight of the two of them together—the strength of the one guarding the innocence and vulnerability of the other—filled Megan with such tenderness and such intense longing that her heart ached.

With his shaggy hair tousled, her ex-husband looked young and sorrow-free again. And Matthew, snuggled into the crook of Jake's muscular arms, was the picture of trusting contentment—as if he knew, instinctively, that no harm would come to him as long as Jake was there.

How well Megan remembered that feeling.

And how very, very much she missed it!

Dear Reader,

Instead of writing your resolutions, I have the perfect way to begin the new year—read this month's spectacular selection of Silhouette Special Edition romances! These exciting books will put a song in your heart, starting with another installment of our very popular MONTANA MAVERICKS series—*In Love With Her Boss* by the stellar Christie Ridgway. Christie vows this year to "appreciate the time I have with my husband and sons and appreciate *them* for the unique people they are."

Lindsay McKenna brings us a thrilling story from her MORGAN'S MERCENARIES: DESTINY'S WOMEN series with *Woman of Innocence*, in which an adventure-seeking beauty meets up with the legendary—and breathtaking—mercenary of her dreams! The excitement continues with Victoria Pade's next tale, *On Pins and Needles*, in her A RANCHING FAMILY series. Here, a skeptical sheriff falls for a lovely acupuncturist who finds the wonder cure for all his doubts—her love!

And what does a small-town schoolteacher do when she finds a baby on her doorstep? Find out in Nikki Benjamin's heartwarming reunion romance *Rookie Cop*. A love story you're sure to savor is *The Older Woman* by Cheryl Reavis, in which a paratrooper captain falls head over heels for the tough-talking nurse living next door. This year, Cheryl wants to "stop and smell the roses." I also recommend Lisette Belisle's latest marriage-of-convenience story, *The Wedding Bargain*, in which an inheritance—and two hearts—are at stake! Lisette believes that the new year means "a fresh start, and vows to meet each new day with renewed faith, energy and a sense of humor."

I'm pleased to celebrate with you the beginning of a brand-new year. May you also stop to smell the roses, and find many treasures in Silhouette Special Edition the whole year through!

Enjoy!

Karen Taylor Richman
Senior Editor

Please address questions and book requests to:
Silhouette Reader Service
U.S.: 3010 Walden Ave., P.O. Box 1325, Buffalo, NY 14269
Canadian: P.O. Box 609, Fort Erie, Ont. L2A 5X3

Rookie Cop

NIKKI BENJAMIN

SPECIAL EDITION™

Published by Silhouette Books

America's Publisher of Contemporary Romance

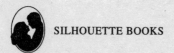 SILHOUETTE BOOKS

ISBN 0-373-24444-4

ROOKIE COP

Visit Silhouette at www.eHarlequin.com

Printed in U.S.A.

Books by Nikki Benjamin

Silhouette Special Edition

Emily's House #539
On the Whispering Wind #663
The Best Medicine #716
It Must Have Been the Mistletoe #782
My Baby, Your Child #880
Only St. Nick Knew #928
The Surprise Baby #1189
The Major and the Librarian #1228
Expectant Bride-To-Be #1368
Rookie Cop #1444

Silhouette Intimate Moments

A Man To Believe In #359
Restless Wind #519
The Wedding Venture #645
The Lady and Alex Payton #729
Daddy by Default #789

NIKKI BENJAMIN

was born and raised in the Midwest, but after years in the Houston area, she considers herself a true Texan. Nikki says she's always been an avid reader. (Her earliest literary heroines were Nancy Drew, Trixie Belden and Beany Malone.) Her writing experience was limited, however, until a friend started penning a novel and encouraged Nikki to do the same. One scene led to another, and soon she was hooked.

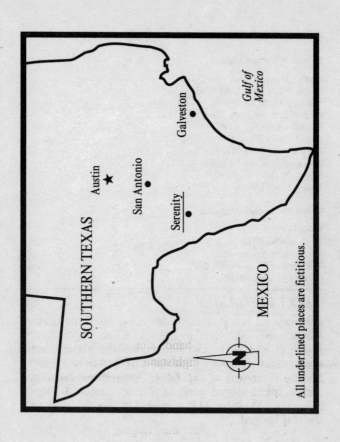

SOUTHERN TEXAS

Austin

San Antonio

Serenity

Galveston

Gulf of
Mexico

MEXICO

N

All underlined places are fictitious.

Chapter One

A shrill ring cut through Megan Cahill's deep, dreamless sleep, drawing her into reluctant wakefulness. Eyes still closed, she responded automatically, reaching out with one hand, aiming to shut off the alarm clock on her nightstand. When her fingers brushed against the solid, fabric-covered cushions lining the back of her living room sofa, she groaned softly, shifted and sat up.

Vaguely aware that the ringing had stopped through no effort of her own, yet still too groggy to place exactly where it had come from, Megan rubbed her bleary eyes. Then she looked around the sparsely furnished living room of the house she had recently bought from her old friend, Emma Dalton Griffin, as she tried to collect her thoughts.

Across the room, the television screen flickered luminously as the host and hostess of an early-morning network talk show bantered back and forth, their low tones much too cheery for her liking. She must have left the television on the night before. Must have fallen asleep in front of it, she thought, eyeing her wrinkled white T-shirt and navy-blue shorts with distaste. Just as she had done so many nights since she had moved back to Serenity, Texas, two years ago.

The shrill ring sounded again, jarring Megan fully awake. Someone was jabbing at her front doorbell with an awfully impatient finger. But why? she wondered. What could anyone want with her so early in the morning?

She couldn't recall making any plans for the day that included anyone except herself. And in the two years she had lived in Serenity, she had avoided making the kind of close friends who would ask for her help in an emergency. Maybe her elderly neighbors, living across the street, needed assistance of some sort. She was on speaking terms with Mr. and Mrs. Bukowski, after all, though only in the most casual sense.

For the third time the doorbell rang, this time followed by a round of urgent knocking on her front door.

"Just a moment," Megan called out, tamping down her momentary annoyance at the unexpected intrusion into her solitary life.

Since returning to Serenity, she had made sure she was beholden to no one and no one was beholden to her. That way she couldn't disappoint anyone, nor would she, herself, be disappointed. It was a lonely way to live, but less painful in the long run. Your illusions couldn't be shattered if you had none.

Someone obviously needed her help, though, and she hadn't shut down her emotions so completely that she could turn the person away without a second thought.

Shoving a hand through the chin-length tangle of dark curls she could never seem to tame, Megan padded toward the front door, the polished wood floor cool against her bare feet. As she turned the key in the bolt lock, she heard the faint shuffle of running footsteps on the porch.

Suddenly realizing that she could be the latest victim of the teenage pranksters who had targeted various other Serenity High School teachers since school had let out for the summer a week ago, Megan flung open the door angrily and stepped outside. Being awakened at the crack of dawn to come to someone's aid was one thing. Being awakened at the crack of dawn just for the fun of it was something else altogether.

With the sun not quite topping the horizon yet, shadows still hovered in the far corners of the wide front porch. A quick glance around assured her that no one was lurking there, though.

Hoping to catch at least a glimpse of whoever had rung her doorbell, then run off, Megan strode toward the short flight of steps leading to the walkway. Looking out across the lawn, she wasn't immediately aware of the baby stroller parked a few feet from the front door. Only the heart-stopping wail of an infant slicing through the early-morning quiet—straight into her soul—made her pause and glance down just in time to prevent what could have been a serious accident.

Megan stared in utter amazement at the tiny, barely discernible form tucked securely into the sturdy, steel-framed, padded canvas stroller. Her heart pounded in her chest and her breath caught in her throat.

"Oh, no... Oh, no, no, no," she whispered as she scanned the front yard again, searching for some sign, *any* sign, of whoever had made the mistake of leaving a baby on her doorstep.

"Come back," she called out urgently, nearly shouting now. "Please, *please,* come back."

Megan didn't try to hide the desperation in her voice—a desperation that clutched at her throat with a frightening stranglehold. Some foolish, misguided person had left a baby on her doorstep. Someone who obviously had no idea what a poor choice they were making. She was the last person on earth to be entrusted with a child's care—the very *last* person on earth.

The twitter of birds greeting the dawn and the baby's increasingly plaintive cries were the only answer to Megan's plea. She was sure that the person who had left the baby on her porch hadn't gone far. But she couldn't leave the baby alone while she went in search of her.

Taking a steadying breath, she set aside her reluctance and bent over the stroller.

"Don't cry, sweetheart," she murmured, the words coming softly, naturally, as they had so often in the past. "Don't cry. Don't cry..."

Reaching down, Megan loosened the pale blue, light cotton blanket covering the infant, then slipped her hands under him, gently cradling his head and bottom as she lifted him from the stroller. His cries faded to little snuffles as she held him close, his downy head nestled under her chin in a way that made her heart ache.

"Ah, sweet Will, sweet little Will. Mommy's here, she's here now...." Megan whispered, though she knew, to the very depths of her soul, that the child she held wasn't *her* child...wasn't her precious Will, and never could be.

Still, her grip on the baby tightened just a little more as she closed her eyes and feathered tiny butterfly kisses along the warm, soft-as-silk curve of his cheek. The weight of his little body, curled against her shoulder, was so solid, so familiar and so very, very *real*. She couldn't help but pretend, for just a moment, that she had taken a step back in time, back to the place where she had once been strong and whole in body, mind and spirit.

The place where she had been all she had ever wanted to be—a wife and a mother.

A rustle in the shrubbery planted along the far end of the porch caught Megan's attention, dragging her back to the present. She heard the distinct thump of feet pounding across the lawn then running down the sidewalk. Holding the baby firmly against her shoulder with both hands, she shoved the stroller out of her way with her hip and scrambled down the porch steps as quickly as she could.

"Don't go," she called out. "Please...don't go."

Megan could barely make out the tall, lithe form skimming away along the sidewalk through the tree-cast shadows. Instinctively, she knew it was a young woman—a young, healthy woman who, for whatever reason, had chosen to leave her baby behind.

By the time Megan finally reached the sidewalk, the woman had disappeared from sight around the distant street corner. Even if she hadn't been holding a baby in her arms, Megan knew she wouldn't have been able to catch up with her. Weighed down as she was, and barefoot to boot, there seemed to be no sense in trying. She would only risk taking a bad fall, and what good would that do?

With a rueful shake of her head, Megan turned and walked back the way she'd come—through the little gate in the white picket fence fronting the yard, along the narrow walkway edged with pink and white impatiens, then up the porch steps.

There had to be a reason why the absconding young woman had chosen to leave her child at 1209 Bay Leaf Lane, she thought. But try as she might, she couldn't come up with one that made the slightest bit of sense to her.

Although she hadn't gotten a good look at the baby yet, she was fairly sure the poor little thing wasn't more than a couple of months old. Of the few people she knew in the small town of Serenity, Texas, none had given birth recently. So who, outside her limited circle of friends—acquaintances, really—would be desperate enough to leave a virtual newborn in her care?

And what, exactly, was she supposed to do now that someone had?

Back on the porch again, Megan crossed to the stroller she had shoved aside a few minutes earlier. With the first rays of sunlight chasing away the shadows, she saw that a quilted denim diaper bag had been left behind, as well. What appeared to be a note with her name written on it in bold block letters had been pinned to one of the straps.

She pulled the single sheet of notebook paper loose with her free hand and unfolded it. The message it held, also printed in bold block letters, was short and to the point, but it did very little to enlighten her.

Mrs. Cahill, the note began. *Please,* please *take care of my baby for me. He is two months old and his name is Matthew.*

Frowning, Megan folded the note again and tucked it into the side pocket of her shorts. Still holding the baby securely against her shoulder, she picked up the diaper bag and plopped it in the stroller. Then she wheeled the stroller into the house.

In the living room, she parked the stroller by the sofa, crossed to the television and turned it off. At the front window, she opened the blinds, letting in the morning sunlight, then returned to the sofa with the baby.

"Okay, let's have a look at you, Matthew."

Perched on the edge of a sofa cushion, Megan gingerly shifted the baby onto her lap. Gazing down at him, she studied him closely. With a downy soft thatch of blond hair, clear, fine-as-porcelain skin and bright blue eyes, he was truly a beautiful baby.

Will had been a beautiful baby, too, but he'd had her dark curls and his father's brown eyes. He had also been more sturdily built than Matthew was. Which had made it all the harder to believe he hadn't been strong enough to fight off the devastating illness that had claimed his life.

Though maybe he would have been if only she had realized sooner—

With a firm mental shake, Megan warned herself to stay focused on the moment at hand. She wouldn't do herself or little Matthew any good by allowing painful memories of a past she couldn't change to overwhelm her now.

Directing all her attention on the baby lying on her lap, she noted that he seemed to be strong and healthy. He kicked his little legs and swung his arms, cooing and gurgling quite contentedly. He also seemed to have been well-cared-for. He not only looked clean, he also smelled clean. And though the pale blue, one-piece cotton knit romper he wore was obviously secondhand, it appeared to be freshly laundered.

Unless Megan was badly mistaken, little Matthew had been looked after with loving tenderness prior to his arrival on her doorstep. Yet he had been abandoned like unwanted baggage.

No, that wasn't really true, Megan admitted, trying to be fair. He had only been left when it was certain that he was safely in her care. And his mother—for surely it had to have been his mother running down the sidewalk—had also left behind a diaper bag, thus making sure that all his immediate needs could be met.

Taking the diaper bag from the stroller, Megan unzipped the top flap and opened it wide. As she fully expected, she found at least a dozen tiny disposable diapers, a container of wet wipes, several cans of formula, two baby bottles with nipples, a box of plastic bottle liners, and several changes of clothes and bibs.

She found nothing more to identify the baby's mother in the diaper bag, though. Nor did the stroller, itself, offer any further revelations. It, too, was obviously secondhand, but of excellent quality and construction.

"So, your mom loves you very much, young man," Megan said, offering her index finger for the baby to grasp. "But she's left you here with me…of all people. Any idea why?"

In response to the sound of her voice, Matthew kicked his legs even faster, then screwed up his darling little face and began to fuss.

"Okay, okay, we'll talk about your mom later," she murmured, shifting sideways on the sofa so she could set him down beside her. "Right now, we'll change your diaper and get you a little something to eat. How does that sound?"

With the supplies provided, Megan replaced Matthew's soggy diaper with a dry one. Then she fished out a can of formula, a bottle and disposable liner from the diaper bag, and with Matthew nestled securely against her shoulder, she headed for the kitchen.

It had been a long time since she had prepared a

baby's bottle single-handedly, but apparently the skill, once learned, was never really forgotten. After a quick warm-up of the bottle, they were back on the living room sofa where Matthew eagerly sucked down the formula in slow, steady gulps.

Watching him, Megan recalled all the times she had fed her own baby in much the same way. She had been able to breast-feed Will, though. Just re-membering the urgent tug of his tiny mouth made her breasts tingle instinctively. He had been such a hearty eater....

Drawing a deep, steadying breath, Megan once again willed away the memories that were still too raw, too painful for her to dwell upon. Recalling, in-stead, the wording of the note she'd stuffed into the pocket of her shorts, she frowned thoughtfully.

Please, please *take care of my baby for me.*

She could think of nothing she would rather do than care for Matthew...today, tomorrow and every day thereafter. Holding him close, inhaling his sweet baby scent as she listened to the soft sounds he made as he nursed, she could almost believe that she had been given a second chance, that she had her own baby back again.

In her heart of hearts, she knew better, though. Just as she also knew that she couldn't allow herself to pretend, even for a few moments, that Matthew was her child to keep.

He had only been left in her care temporarily. He had a mother. A mother who would surely come back for him before too long.

Matthew had been cared for with such obvious consideration that Megan couldn't believe he had been casually abandoned on her doorstep. His mother had wanted him to be safe and secure, and for reasons yet to be determined, she had chosen Megan to look out for him. But only until she was able to provide for him again herself.

Becoming too attached to him in the meantime would be a big mistake. She had lost one child. She wasn't about to set herself up for the pain of losing another.

As she had when she'd first found the baby on her front porch, Megan wondered who Matthew's mother might be. Again, she had to admit that she had no idea at all. Nor did she have any idea why *she* had been chosen to provide his safekeeping. Surely his mother must know other women in Serenity more capable of caring for a baby. Women his mother had to know better than she knew Megan Cahill.

When Matthew finished the last of the formula in his bottle, Megan set it aside, lifted him to her shoulder and gently patted his back. He rewarded her with a series of hearty burps, making her smile. Then he snuggled against her with a tiny, contented yawn.

"What a good baby you are," she murmured, brushing her lips against the top of his downy head. "What a good, good baby…"

As she continued to pat his back, Matthew stuck one little fist in his mouth and closed his eyes.

"So, you're ready for a nap, are you?" she asked. "And here I thought you could give me some idea of what we should do next. She's your mother, after all. Do you think we ought to wait here in case she decides to come back for you? Or should we turn you over to the proper authorities without delay?

"I'm tempted to wait here for a while, sweet baby—so very, very tempted. But I'm not really the best person to look after you, no matter what your mother thinks. How about giving her an hour or two? Then I think we'd better take a little walk to the police station."

Matthew's deep, even breathing was the only reply Megan received.

"Okay, that's what we'll do, then," she decided as she stood and headed for the staircase leading to the second floor of the house.

In fact, the Serenity police station was the last place Megan wanted to go that morning. Under the circumstances, however, it was also the best place she could go. That was where she would most likely find the one person capable of helping her track down Matthew's mother.

Unfortunately, Serenity's chief of police, Jake Cahill, also happened to be her ex-husband.

Megan had been avoiding Jake ever since he had returned to Serenity a year ago. He had given up a rewarding career as an FBI agent to take a job that he couldn't possibly find fulfilling. A gesture of reconciliation, or so he had seemed to have wanted her to believe. But it had been too little, much, *much* too late. As she had told him plainly the one time he had come to the house to see her.

Jake had abandoned her when she had needed him the most, just as her parents had done when she was a child. They hadn't thought twice about flying off to a Third World country to cover a military coup, and she'd been left an orphan. And Jake hadn't thought twice about going undercover for weeks at a time to catch a killer, leaving her to cope alone with a sick child.

Megan knew she hadn't occupied a very important place in her parents' lives. Too late, she had realized, as well, that she—and Will—hadn't occupied a very important place in Jake's life, either.

Leaving Jake had been the only way she'd been able to cope with that knowledge. And shutting him out when he finally followed her back to Serenity had been the only way she could keep from falling under his spell again.

She had loved him once—loved him and trusted him with all her heart. She hadn't been about to let him lure her into doing it again, no matter how sad and lonely she had been without him in her life.

While Megan couldn't allow herself to trust Jake personally, she knew, however, that as a law enforcement officer she could trust him to look out for Matthew's best interests. After all, Jake, like her parents, had always put his job first.

At the top of the stairs, Megan paused and eyed the closed door of the bedroom she had studiously ignored since moving into the house she'd rented, partially furnished, from her friend and former foster sister, Emma, just two years ago.

When Emma and her husband, air force colonel Sam Griffin, had moved to Colorado Springs, Megan had arranged to have most of Emma's furniture shipped to them. But Emma had asked Megan to donate the baby furniture in the spare room to one of the local churches, a task that Megan was still unable to take on.

Believing that someone less fortunate than she might benefit from her loss, thus making that loss a little easier to bear, she had given away Will's baby furniture before moving back to Serenity. Standing quietly, watching as her precious child's belongings had been carried out of the town house, she'd felt as if her heart was being ripped from her chest. Supervising the removal of another crib, dresser and changing table had been more than she could bring herself to do.

Now, as fate would have it, she had a crib all ready for Matthew. Well, not exactly *ready*. After months of neglect, the spare room was too musty and dusty for a baby. And it would be foolish to take the time to tidy it up when she would only be responsible for him another hour or so at the most.

Putting Matthew down on her bed, with pillows on either side of him serving as bolsters, would be much easier, she decided, moving past the closed door. And if he began to fuss while she took a shower, she would be better able to hear him if he were in her bedroom.

Better to keep things as simple as possible, and to remain matter-of-fact, Megan reminded herself. By afternoon, the baby would either be reunited with his mother or placed under the care of one of the social workers assigned to the county's Children's Protective Services while Jake began an investigation of some sort.

As for her, she'd be home again with a new curriculum to plan for her Texas history class at Serenity High School.

Settling Matthew in the center of her bed, then arranging the pillows around him in a protective circle, Megan smiled sadly. He was such a good, sweet baby. But he wasn't *her* baby, and he never would be.

Chapter Two

"I told you I'd think about your offer, Bobby, and I've been doing just that. But I haven't made a decision yet," Jake Cahill stated firmly.

Sitting back in his chair, he propped one boot-shod foot on the edge of his desk. Beyond the window in the wall separating his small office from the rest of the Serenity police station all appeared to be quiet. It was a typical small-town Friday morning early in the month of June.

"We need you back on our team, and the sooner the better," Bobby Fuentes insisted. "I've got a place for you now, but I can't guarantee how much longer I'll be able to hold it open. We've been working shorthanded for over two months now. I'm starting to get some flack from the higher-ups."

"Find somebody else, then," Jake replied, mildly reproving.

There had been a time when he wouldn't have even dared to think about using such a tone with Bobby. As special agent in charge of the Federal Bureau of Investigation's Dallas office, the older man had been Jake's immediate, and demanding, supervisor for several years. He had also become a good friend and respected mentor.

Even now, more than a year after he'd left the FBI, Jake knew that Bobby only had his best interests at heart. But he refused to be bullied. He had too much at stake to make a hasty decision, especially one that would affect his future in such a conclusive way.

"Problem is, I want you," Bobby continued, apparently choosing to ignore Jake's suggestion. "Our arrest records and conviction rates haven't been the same since you left the bureau. And don't tell me you're satisfied playing at being the chief of police in a place like Serenity, Texas. Talk about wasted talent."

"I *am* the chief of police—no playing about it," Jake shot back, bristling at the sarcasm he'd heard in his old friend's voice.

He hadn't resigned from the FBI and returned to Serenity on a whim. He had wanted desperately to win back the love and trust of his ex-wife, Megan, and he'd known of no other way to do it than by following her back to their hometown. Sure that it would only be a matter of time before she allowed him back into her life, Jake had asked his father, William Cahill—an honored member of the Texas leg-islature and one of Serenity's most highly regarded citizens—to pull whatever strings were necessary to get him on the town's police force.

Never one for half measures, especially where his only son was concerned, Senator Cahill had person-ally taken it upon himself to urge the aging chief of police to accept an early retirement package that in-cluded benefits no man in his right mind could refuse. Then he nominated Jake to take the chief's place. The town fathers, aware that they were getting a darn good deal, had been delighted to smooth the way for the senator's son. And over the past year Jake had taken great pride in seeing to it that they weren't disap-pointed.

"Hey, no offense meant," Bobby hastened to as-sure him.

"Difficult as it might be for a big-city guy like you to believe, I happen to like Serenity. I grew up here, you know. It's a nice place to live and a great place to raise a family."

"Speaking of which, are you and Megan on speak-ing terms yet? It's been, what, two years since she left you? Maybe it's time to cut bait, old buddy. You can't spend the rest of your life waiting for something to happen when you have to know by now that the odds are against it. Some marriages can survive the kind of loss you and Megan suffered. Yours didn't. You would do best to put it behind you, once and for all, and get on with your life."

Bringing his foot down on the floor again, Jake

shifted in his chair, sat up straighter and shoved a hand through his dark, shaggy hair. Bobby's words hit painfully close to the mark, ripping at the battered edges of his heart as they laid forth a truth he would have rather not been forced to face.

Jake had made his fair share of mistakes over the years, but the ones he'd made with Megan seemed destined to haunt him for the rest of his life. He shouldn't have put his job first three years ago, leaving her alone and unable to reach him when their young son began running a high fever. Nor should he have used his job as a means of escaping the grief and guilt that had threatened to overwhelm him after the meningitis that was diagnosed too late claimed Will's life. And finally, fatally for their marriage, he shouldn't have waited so long to follow Megan back to Serenity.

He had told himself that she simply needed time away from their home in Dallas and the memories of Will it held for her. That had been what he had thought he'd needed, after all. Only when she filed for divorce did he realize that she wasn't coming back to him.

Fool that he'd been, he had told himself he didn't really care. Eventually, of course, he'd come to his senses, but by then, Megan had made a new life for herself. A life that very likely might never include him.

"My relationship with Megan is none of your business, Bobby, so just back the hell off," Jake warned, the memories he'd had of the past making him as angry with himself as he was with his old friend.

"Sorry if I was out of line, but I was just trying to point out what seems obvious to everyone except you. You dealt with Will's death the only way you knew how and Megan dealt with it her way."

"Because I gave her no other choice," Jake retorted. "I wasn't there for her when she really needed me. When Will first got sick I was too anxious to start working on yet another high-profile case to stick around and give her the support she needed. And after he died, it was easier for me to hide from her pain as well as my own by using any excuse I could to stay as far away from home as possible.

"I let her down, Bobby—no two ways about it. I was all she had and I let her down, and then I lost her. I lost the best thing in my life—the *two* best things—my wife and my son. I know I'll never be able to get Will back. But I'm not ready to admit that Megan won't ever be a part of my life again, either. As soon as I am, I'll let you know."

Without waiting for a last comment from his friend, Jake hung up the phone, then pressed the heels of his hands against his eyes in an effort to ease the subtle pressure that warned of a full-blown headache on the way.

As he had so many times already, he thought back over the months that had passed since he'd first returned to Serenity, and tried to figure out what he'd been doing wrong. He wanted his wife back. But he wasn't any closer to his goal than he'd been a year ago.

Jake didn't want to have to resort to force to get Megan to listen to what he had to say. But lately he had begun to think that hauling her off to some secluded place and holding her captive might not be such a bad idea, after all.

He had tried to consider her feelings—heaven help him, how he'd tried. For months now he'd been so busy tying himself up in knots worrying about making the wrong moves that he hadn't made any moves at all. In fact, she had shut the door in his face the one and only time he'd attempted to confront her face-to-face.

Wincing as he remembered that particularly disheartening exchange, Jake sat back in his chair again.

He had gone to her house one Saturday morning nine months ago. She had opened the door without hesitation, and she'd met his gaze quite calmly. She'd offered him no greeting, though. Standing just inside the doorway, dressed in faded jeans and a plain white T-shirt, her dark curls a tantalizing tangle begging to be touched, she'd simply looked at him, her chin tipped up defensively, her wide, pale gray eyes filled with reproach.

Not a single one of the casual, clever opening lines Jake had rehearsed had come to his mind. He hadn't been so close to her in such a long, lonely time— close enough to feel the heat radiating from her body, close enough to breathe in her special scent.

Lavender, he'd thought, every nerve ending in his body tingling with awareness.

He had wanted only to put his arms around her, to hold her close and feather kisses along her cheek as he begged for her forgiveness.

He had known that she wouldn't let him touch her, though. Known it with a certainty that had made his heart ache. But surely she would listen to what he had to say....

"I need to talk to you, Megan," he'd begun, his voice rasping in his throat.

"Oh, really?" she had replied, the look in her eyes changing to one of utter disdain.

"Yes, really. Please, just let me come in. Give me a chance—"

"The time for talking has passed, Jake," she'd said, her tone ever so polite as she cut him off.

Her gaze never wavering, she had closed the door in his face with a finality that had sliced straight through to his soul.

Since that long-ago day, Megan had ignored him every time he'd arranged for their paths to cross at one public place or another. In fact, the studious way in which she avoided any contact with him had not only become cause for comment in the close-knit community, it had also reached laughable proportions.

Jake had wanted to give Megan the time and space she seemed to need. But for all the glimpses of him he had made sure she'd catch around town, she hadn't warmed up to him in the least. The time had come to take more vigorous action.

Now all he had to do was think of some way, short of kidnapping her, to gain her complete and undivided attention. And then, of course, he would have to find the words to tell her how very sorry he was for letting her down—words that he had no way of making her believe.

Closing his eyes again, Jake tried rubbing his temples, pressing hard in a futile attempt to ease the throb in his head.

Megan seemed happy enough with the life she had made for herself in Serenity. Maybe she didn't really want him around anymore, and he was simply failing to take the hint. And maybe, just maybe, the rumors he'd heard about a new man in her life were actually true.

Though Jake had yet to see Megan and Steven Barns—the high school principal who had lost his wife almost two years ago—together himself, he had it on good authority that they had danced quite a few times at the senior prom they'd chaperoned. They had also shared a table at the school picnic.

Jake ground his teeth at the thought of good old Steve, one of the town's designated nice guys, putting his hands on Megan. She might not be his wife anymore, but that didn't mean he—

A subtle but noticeable shift in the atmosphere outside his office caught Jake's attention. The activity level in the station had been fairly low, but until a moment ago, the steady drone of voices—two of his younger officers kidding around with Darcy Osgood, the clerk who maintained the files and answered the phones—had been audible. The sudden, unexpected silence was deafening by comparison.

Turning in his chair, Jake glanced out the window in his office wall to see what was going on, then all but doubled over at the painful lurch that sucked the air from his lungs as it grabbed at his gut.

As if conjured by the force of his thoughts and memories, Megan walked slowly toward his office, weaving her way among the scattered desks as his officers and Darcy looked on in surprised silence. And she was holding a baby in her arms—an infant hardly more than a couple of months old.

Flung back to another time in another place, Jake recalled all too vividly watching Megan walk toward him just so, her gaze turned inward, her mouth softening with a tender smile as her cheek brushed their son's dark curls. Slashing through him as they did, the knife thrust of those memories, shut away for so long, made it momentarily impossible for him to draw a breath, to push away from his desk, to stand and close the distance still between them.

Get up and go to her and find out what the hell is going on, he ordered himself, aware that he had to gather himself quickly and take control of the situation, not only for his sake but for Megan's, as well. She wouldn't have come to him unless she needed his help—needed it desperately.

Jake couldn't seem to make his legs work, though. Couldn't seem to find the strength to stand and meet her halfway. In an effort to steady his roiling thoughts and emotions, he shifted his gaze from Megan.

He saw that she had left a stroller parked near the station doorway. He also saw that Darcy and his officers were gawking at her curiously. When he shot a pointed glance at them, they moved hurriedly to their respective desks and pretended to busy themselves with paperwork, and he allowed himself another look at Megan.

She was almost at the door to his office, but she seemed intent only on watching where she was walking. As if she preferred not to acknowledge his presence until the last possible moment, even though she could be there for no other reason than to see him.

She was dressed just as she had been that day nine months ago when he'd gone to see her, in faded jeans and a plain white T-shirt that emphasized how thin she'd gotten over the past few years. Too thin, he thought. And today she was also far too pale for his liking. Against the artful disarray of her dark, chin-length tumble of curls, her face had an almost ghostly cast.

Whatever the reason behind her sudden, unexpected arrival at the Serenity police station, baby in her arms, she was noticeably upset by it. And so, by association, was he, Jake admitted, finally pushing his chair away from his desk so he could stand.

He had wanted to believe that they had each put the death of their son behind them—he in his way and Megan in hers. Now he realized how mistaken he'd been. From the look of her, Megan had to have been jolted as surely as he by the mere sight of the baby she held so protectively. A baby that had to be for her, as it was for him, a living, breathing reminder of all they'd lost.

As Megan paused just inside his office doorway, Jake started toward her, bumping a hip against the edge of his desk hard enough to make him wince.

"Megan…?" he began, his voice sounding harsher to him than intended as he tried to gain some control over his unsteady emotions. "What's going on?"

Raising her head slowly, she met his gaze at last, the wariness in her icy gray eyes halting him in mid-step. She couldn't have told him more succinctly how much she regretted having to be there with him if she'd said the words out loud. The message radiated from her very core, coming at him in an almost tangible wave meant to keep him at a distance—as it did.

Jake shoved his hands in the pockets of his khaki pants, mentally cursing himself for thinking, as he had for just a moment, of reaching out to her, putting an arm around her shoulders and drawing her close to his side. She hadn't come to him seeking comfort, and she wouldn't appreciate the offer of it. Not by a long shot….

"I need your help," she answered with just the slightest hesitation, her voice surprisingly cool and utterly, completely detached.

Only the pulse beat of a vein at her temple hinted at her apprehension. Coming to him was costing her much more than she was willing to admit, Jake knew. But come to him she had, and he had nothing to gain by giving her a hard time. In fact, he might be able to win some much needed points by smoothing the way for her as best he could.

"I'm here to serve and protect," he said, lightening his tone considerably as he offered her a wry smile. "Just tell me what I can do for you, and consider it done."

The wariness in Megan's eyes deepened almost imperceptibly, warning him anew that she wasn't about to be easily tempted to lower her guard. He had been just a tad too genial and she hadn't been favorably impressed.

"An odd thing happened this morning," she said after another moment's hesitation. Then she glanced away with seeming uncertainty.

"Would I be correct in assuming it has something to do with your young friend there?" Jake prompted gently.

He knew that it did, of course. But a nudge in the right direction might make it easier for her to give him an explanation.

Megan nodded her head, then met his gaze again. As she did, Jake saw that the wariness in her eyes had been replaced by a pleading look that caught him off guard. When she spoke again, her tone had also changed, revealing the agitation she had, up until then, succeeded in hiding from him.

"Someone left him on my front porch," she blurted out. "Just *left* him in a stroller. His name is Matthew, and he seems to be healthy. He's obviously been well-cared-for, too. Whoever left him, left diapers and formula and clean clothes for him in a diaper

bag. And a note—a note addressed to me personally—asking me to take care of him.'' She sighed. ''I
want to do that. More than anything, I want to take
care of him. But I know I can't. Not the way she
meant. I can't just pretend he's mine and go about
my business. I have to turn him over to the proper
authorities.

''That's why I'm here. To turn him over to Children's Protective Services. And to ask you, please, to
see if you can find his mother. I'm afraid she's in
some kind of trouble. Otherwise, why would she
leave her baby with me?''

Her voice breaking suddenly, Megan ducked her
head again, but not before Jake saw the glimmer of
tears in her eyes. He closed the distance between them
then, her misery lodging deep in his own heart. Lim-
iting himself to just a light touch on her shoulder so
as not to upset her any further, he guided her to one
of the two chairs positioned in front of his desk as he
tried to make sense of all that she'd told him.

''Let me make sure I understand the situation,'' he
said after she'd settled into the chair and drawn a
steadying breath. ''This morning someone, most
probably the mother, left the baby you're holding on
your front porch?''

''Yes, unbelievable as it sounds, that's exactly what
happened,'' Megan replied.

Against her shoulder, the baby squirmed and snuf-
fled, then snuggled back to sleep as she smoothed a
soothing hand down his back.

Seeing how naturally she mothered the abandoned

infant, Jack ached for her even more. She was determined to do the right thing, to give up the baby to Children's Protective Services, but she'd said herself it wasn't what she wanted to do. Her tenderness toward the baby made it even more evident.

Telling himself he could help Megan best by setting aside his own feelings and doing his job, Jake stepped back, propped a hip on the edge of his desk and picked up his notebook and pen. He didn't want to crowd her, but at the same time, he didn't want to put the width of his desk between them, either.

Finding herself caught in a situation that had to be almost too painful for her to bear, she was barely hanging on, riding a roller coaster of emotions. Yet she'd had the courage and the common sense to come to him for help. He didn't want her to think that he would let her down, even for a moment. Not this time, no matter what hell he had to go through himself.

"What time was it when you found him?" he asked, trying to keep his tone matter-of-fact as he opened his notebook and jotted down the date on a fresh page.

"Just after dawn." Megan drew another steadying breath and met his gaze, her composure somewhat restored. "I fell asleep on the living room sofa last night and woke up this morning to the sound of the doorbell ringing. I was pretty sure it was just kids from the high school playing a prank. I went to the door and opened it to be sure they hadn't left behind any little gifts. Nobody was there, of course. I stepped out on the porch to take a look around the yard, and almost tripped over the stroller. Luckily, he started to cry and I saw him just in time.''

"You seem fairly sure that his *mother* is the one who left him there. Why is that?''

''Instinct, mostly. I had a feeling that he hadn't been abandoned completely, that someone was close by, watching to make sure he was okay. I called out, asking her to please come back. As I started down the porch steps, I heard a rustle in the shrubbery alongside the house, and a few moments later, I saw someone running down the sidewalk.''

"Can you give me a description of her?'' Jake asked, eyeing her questioningly.

''Not in any great detail,'' Megan admitted. ''It wasn't light enough outside, and she was running pretty fast. I had taken the baby out of the stroller and was holding him, so I couldn't really go after her. I'm sure it was a young woman, though. She was tall and slender, she was wearing jeans and a T-shirt, and she had her hair tucked under a baseball cap.''

Tapping his pen against his notebook, Jake frowned thoughtfully. He had seen someone dressed much the same way as Megan's early-morning visitor when he was heading to work around seven o'clock. She had been walking away from the Serenity bus station.

He, too, had assumed the jeans-clad figure was a young woman. He hadn't paid her much attention, but then, he hadn't had any reason to. Just another college student home for the summer, he'd mused, eyeing the loaded duffel bag and backpack weighing her down.

Unfortunately, he hadn't gotten a good look at her

face, either. And thanks to the baseball cap she'd worn, he couldn't have said if her hair was short or long, dark or fair.

"What are you thinking?" Megan asked, her tone soft and tentative.

"I saw her this morning, too," Jake answered. "Around seven o'clock, apparently after she'd been to your house. She was leaving the bus station, carrying a duffel bag and backpack. I assumed she was a college student home for the summer."

"That would mean she has family here in town, wouldn't it? So why leave her baby with me?"

"That's what I need to find out. Do you have the note she left with the baby?"

"It's in the diaper bag hooked onto the handle of the stroller. I brought everything she left so you could take a look at it. CPS will want his things, too." Megan hesitated, shifting her gaze away. "I guess you'd better call over there and ask them to send a social worker to take him."

Jake couldn't help but notice how her grip on the baby tightened imperceptibly, and his heart ached for her even more. Talk about a rotten set of circumstances. She shouldn't have had to deal with something as agonizing as finding an abandoned baby on her front porch. Not after the loss she had suffered almost three years ago. The loss *they* had suffered.

For one long moment, Jake wished he had the power to whisk her, the baby and himself back in time so they could be a family again—he, Megan and their own sweet Will. As if to remind him of how impossible his fantasy was, the baby started to fuss, his snuffling cries an obvious supplication.

"He's probably hungry again," Megan said by way of explanation. "There's a bottle of formula in the diaper bag. Would you run it under some hot water for me for a minute?"

"Sure thing."

Glad to have a task that not only took his mind off the past, but also grounded him firmly in the present, Jake hurried out of his office. He asked one of the young officers to call Children's Protective Services for him and request that a social worker be sent to the police station at once. Then he walked back to the stroller, found the bottle of formula in the diaper bag and headed for the station's small kitchen. Along the way, he paused to ask Darcy to wheel the stroller back to his office just in case the baby also needed a change of diaper.

By the time he made his way back to his office, warm bottle in hand, the baby's cries had increased in volume. Megan paced the narrow space in front of his desk, patting the infant's back and murmuring words of reassurance while Darcy looked on sympathetically from the doorway.

"Phone's ringing," Jake said, shooting her a reproving look as he walked past her.

"I'd better answer it, then." Obviously regretting what she would be missing, Darcy backed out of the office and headed for her desk.

Taking the bottle Jake held out to her, Megan spared him a grateful glance, then sank into her chair again, shifted the baby in her arms and offered him the bottle. He quieted immediately, latching onto the nipple and sucking greedily.

As he hovered just inside the doorway, Jake was hit yet again by a twist of pain deep in his gut. Watching Megan, her attention focused solely on the baby, brought back even more memories he couldn't bear to face. The longing in his former wife's eyes, the tender curve of her lips, the whisper-soft nonsense she spoke to the child in her arms had him turning on his heel and walking away, hands clenched at his sides.

He wasn't sure which was harder to quell—the urge to rage at the heavens or the urge to sob his heart out. Somehow he made it back to the tiny kitchen without doing either. Somehow he filled a paper cup with water and gulped it down. Somehow he managed to breathe again, and to wipe away the lone tear trickling down his cheek before Darcy bustled in to tell him that Alice Radford from CPS had arrived.

Chapter Three

Though she had most of her attention focused on Matthew as he nursed greedily from the bottle, Megan was aware of the exact moment when Jake left her alone in his office. She also had a pretty good idea of why he had fled in such an obvious hurry.

She'd seen the anguish in his eyes when she first met his gaze, and she had known then that she wasn't the only one doing battle with painful memories— memories stirred by the sweet baby she held in her arms. And they were both dealing with those memories in the same way they had dealt with the reality of Will's death.

She had faced her sorrow squarely while doing, on her own, what needed to be done. And Jake, obviously unable to admit to face the depth of his pain, had gone off to immerse himself in his work.

Megan wasn't surprised by his sudden desertion. After all, he was only behaving true to form. She would have been foolish to expect anything else of him. As for her disappointment, that was of her own making. She shouldn't have allowed herself to entertain even the slightest illusion that Jake would grieve with her over the memory of their young son any more than he had grieved with her over Will's death.

But seeing him again, up close and personal—looking fit and trim in khaki pants and a white shirt, sleeves rolled to his elbows, his dark, shaggy hair softening his hawkish features, his brown-eyed gaze warm and direct—had stirred a longing in her for days past. A longing that had brought with it memories of all the hopes and dreams of happily ever after she had so staunchly set aside when she'd left him two years ago.

Over and over again as Megan had answered Jake's questions about the baby, she'd had to remind herself that she'd come to him on Matthew's behalf, not her own, and then only because she trusted him to do his job, nothing more.

She didn't dare allow herself to think anything else. Nor could she allow her heart to soften toward him even the tiniest bit. She would end up being hurt all over again, and that she could definitely do without.

Aware that Matthew was watching her with his big blue eyes as he finished the last of the formula in the bottle, Megan smiled down at him. She should be enjoying what time she had with him instead of letting thoughts of Jake get her down. He was such a good baby and he seemed so content. He didn't fuss at all when she set the bottle aside, shifted him to her shoulder and gently patted his back.

Will had been a good baby, too, she remembered. Such a good, good baby—

"Well, what have we here?"

Drawn from her reverie by the sound of a familiar feminine voice coming from Jake's office doorway, Megan glanced over her shoulder. The baby lifted his head, too, obviously curious, and let loose a gurgling burp.

"Hello, Alice," Megan said, smiling at the social worker she had first met several months ago. "It's good to see you again."

"It's good to see you again, too, Megan." Alice Radford returned her smile as she stepped into the office and set her briefcase on Jake's desk. Though dressed conservatively in tailored black pants and a black-and-white striped shirt, she wore her iron gray hair cut short and spiked with mousse. And she fairly bristled with energy as she added, "*Very* good, under the circumstances."

"You two know each other?" Jake asked as he paused just inside the doorway.

"Oh, yes," Alice answered, her gaze settling intently on the baby. "Meg completed CPS's training program for prospective foster parents just three weeks ago, and a good thing, too."

From the corner of her eye, Megan saw Jake glance her way, a frown creasing his forehead. She only had a moment to wonder what he must be thinking. Then Alice demanded her full attention again as she held out her hands for the baby.

"Jake filled me in on the details of how you ended up with this little guy. And you have no idea at all who the mother might be?"

"None," Megan replied, experiencing an odd mixture of reluctance and relief as Alice took Matthew from her.

He wasn't her baby, but in the all-too-short time she had cared for him since she'd found him on her front porch, he had wiggled his way into her heart. For whatever reason, he had been entrusted to her care. Even with Alice ready to take over for her, she couldn't quite set aside the feeling that she was still responsible for his well-being.

Not that the social worker was being anything but gentle as she looked Matthew over with a practiced eye. And she would make absolutely sure that he was placed with a kind and loving foster family.

"He seems healthy enough, and he doesn't appear to be neglected in any way," Alice stated. "No signs of physical abuse, either—at least none that I can see."

"None that I could see, either," Megan agreed.

"We'll have to stop by the hospital with him and let one of the staff pediatricians give him a thorough checkup just to be sure. Then we can stop by my office, fill out the necessary paperwork, and he's yours."

Alice held the baby out to Megan and she took him without hesitation. When the social worker's last words sank in, however, she stared at the woman, unable to hide her dismay.

"Mine?" she asked, her voice high and tight.

"You're fully qualified to foster young Matthew," Alice assured her, waving a dismissive hand.

Megan wasn't heartened in the least by the social worker's statement. Granted, she had gone through the foster parenting program offered by the county, but only so she could provide a home for older children, especially siblings who might be separated otherwise. A home similar to the one where she'd been placed in Serenity after her parents had been killed.

She hadn't expected to be asked to care for a baby, mainly because they were so much easier to place within the foster care system. She also had a full-time job teaching history at the high school. Caring for older, school-age children made more sense since her schedule would coincide with theirs, allowing her to be at home when they were.

But school was out for the summer, and if Alice really needed her...

"Surely there's someone available who's much more experienced than I am," Megan insisted, trying, unsuccessfully, to ignore the all-too-familiar way the baby snuggled against her shoulder.

It was hard enough for her to accept the fact that Matthew wasn't her baby to keep now. But after days, perhaps even weeks, of looking after him, the pain of letting him go would be unbearable.

"Once you've completed our program, you're qualified to care for children of any age. And right now we're woefully shorthanded. We need you, Megan. *Matthew* needs you."

Oh, great, just what *she* needed, Megan thought to herself. A little none-too-subtle yet oh-so-gentle coercion from one of the few people in town she truly liked.

"Unless, of course, you foresee having a serious problem with him," Alice added, pinning her with a questioning look.

"Not at all," Megan assured her, aware that she'd just sealed her own fate. But why argue any longer against something she wanted so much?

In the doorway, Jake shifted, drawing her attention. A frown still creasing his forehead, he looked none too happy at the sudden turn of events. Megan couldn't even begin to imagine what must have been going through his head as he'd listened to her verbal exchange with Alice.

Of course, his thoughts shouldn't really matter to her. He wasn't a part of her life anymore. Her agreement to care for Matthew had nothing to do with him. His job began and ended with finding the baby's mother.

"Good." Alice nodded once, then added briskly, "You'll need a crib for him. We have a Portacrib at the office you can use. And I already have a car seat for him out in my van."

"Actually, I have a crib at the house," Megan said, then immediately regretted the admission as she saw Jake straighten in the doorway, a puzzled look on his face.

During one of his rare breaks from the case he'd been working on after Will's death, he had come home to find that the room they'd used as the baby's nursery was standing empty. He hadn't said a word when she told him she'd donated all of Will's things to charity. The following day, he'd left again, and a few days after that, she had headed back to Serenity.

"Emma left it there," she explained, glancing at Jake. "It belonged to Jane Hamilton originally. I meant to have one of the local charities come and get it, but I never got around to it."

In the two years I've lived in the house hung unspoken between them.

"Well, now that you're part of our foster care program that crib is going to come in handy, isn't it?" Alice interjected smoothly, her smile laced with satisfaction. "I knew we were lucky to have you sign on, Meg. Now I realize what a godsend you're truly going to be." Alice retrieved her briefcase from Jake's desk, then latched a hand onto one of the stroller's handles. "So, hospital first, if you're ready."

"I think I'd better change his diaper before we go," Megan advised, wrinkling her nose a bit to make her point.

"By all means." Alice grinned. "I've got a couple of calls to make. Mind if I use one of your phones, Jake?"

"Not at all." Jake backed out of the doorway so Alice could pass by, then walked with her to Darcy's desk.

Alone with the baby in the station's rest room, Megan lowered the back of the stroller's seat so Matthew could lie flat on it. He squirmed and kicked his legs, looking as if he was getting ready to cry.

"Just give me a minute and I'll get rid of that poopy old diaper for you," she murmured, taking a fresh disposable from the diaper bag along with the container of wet wipes.

Matthew quieted immediately as Megan tended to him, once again watching her with his big blue eyes. Megan smiled at him, then hesitated, cocking her head to one side as she heard voices coming from just outside the rest room door.

"His ex-wife…" Darcy said. "He followed her back to Serenity almost a year ago. Quit the FBI and had his father pull all kinds of strings to get him on as chief of police."

"He *quit* the FBI to come back *here?*"

The masculine voice must belong to one of the young officers she had seen when she first arrived at the police station, Megan thought as she listened guiltily to a conversation that certainly wasn't meant for her ears.

"Yeah, and all for nothing," Darcy replied. "They haven't gotten together, and probably never will. So he's thinking about going back to the FBI. Some guy named Bobby Fuentes, *Special Agent* Bobby Fuentes, has been calling him at least once a week for a couple of months now—"

"Hey, I think the chief wants me," the officer interrupted. "Thanks for filling me in, though."

"No problem."

In the sudden silence, Megan slowly secured the tabs on Matthew's diaper. Her mind racing, she quickly washed her hands at the sink. Then she raised the stroller seat and strapped the baby into place for the walk out to Alice's car.

So, Jake had been talking to his former boss,

Bobby Fuentes, about going back to the bureau. Only the fact that he had waited so long caused her surprise. He had lasted at least six months longer than she'd expected as Serenity's chief of police.

What Megan wasn't prepared for, however, was the utter sense of dismay that had grabbed at her gut when she'd realized his departure could be imminent. There was regret, too, though she couldn't say why. She had made it clear that she wanted nothing more to do with him almost a year ago. He had betrayed her love and trust once. She had no intention of giving him a chance to do it again.

But his presence in Serenity had given her a feeling of security. Somewhere in the back of her mind, she had known, for almost twelve months now, that she could go to him in an emergency, just as she had today, and he would help her in any way he could. As long as he didn't have to get too close to anything that might cause him pain...

Reminded of the very reason why she had left Jake in the first place, Megan slung the diaper bag over her shoulder and wheeled the stroller out of the rest room. She leveled her gaze at Alice Radford, waiting for her at the station doorway, and forced herself to smile with confidence she didn't really feel.

"All ready if you are," she said.

"Perfect timing. My van is parked out front." Alice nodded to Jake, standing off to one side. "Nice to see you again, Chief Cahill."

"Alice." He nodded, too.

Megan risked a quick glance at him and saw that he was watching her, his expression unreadable.

Again she found herself wondering what he was thinking, and again she reminded herself that it didn't matter.

"Thanks for your help, Jake," she said, smiling at him, as well, though she didn't meet his gaze.

"You're welcome, Megan," he replied, then added much too smoothly for her peace of mind, "I'll stop by your house later and let you know what I find out about the baby's mother."

"Fine."

She sailed past him without a backward glance, pushing the stroller ahead of her. She could only hope she'd hidden the flash of panic she'd felt when he'd mentioned seeing her later. She didn't want him stopping by her house tonight or any night. But telling him so, especially under the circumstances, would have been downright boorish.

Pausing on the sidewalk next to Alice's van a few moments later, Megan drew a steadying breath, then bent to unfasten the straps holding Matthew in place. She was going to have to work with Jake to find Matthew's mother, no two ways about it. She might as well get used to the idea, and the sooner, the better.

When Megan straightened again, holding him in her arms, she caught Alice eyeing her quizzically.

"What?" she asked uncertainly.

"You and Jake." Alice shrugged and shook her head. "When you speak to each other, you're so cool...so polite. But when you look at each other..." Again she shook her head, obviously bemused. "I know it's none of my business, but have you two considered getting back together? You obviously still care a great deal about each other.''

Like almost everyone in town, Alice had to know some, if not all, of Megan and Jake's past history. And like almost everyone in town, she also seemed to have an opinion about their current situation. An opinion she obviously thought Megan needed to hear.

Staring straight at the social worker, Megan tipped her chin up and made *her* opinion known, as well.

''Not in a million years,'' she said. ''Not in a million, trillion years.''

Alice smiled slightly, making no effort to hide her disbelief, then shrugged again. ''Whatever you say, dear. But methinks the lady protests too much.''

Unable to conjure any further comment that would dissuade Alice from her belief, Megan lifted Matthew out of the stroller and strapped him into the car seat. Obviously having fired her best shot, Alice folded the stroller and stashed it in the back of her van, then climbed behind the steering wheel as Megan settled into the passenger seat.

''Off we go,'' Alice said, starting the engine.

''Yes, indeed,'' Megan agreed, forcing herself to smile despite the sudden, almost overwhelming sense of panic that squeezed at her chest.

As she rode along with Alice, her hands clasped tightly in her lap, she began to realize the full extent of what she'd done, not to mention the repercussions that would follow. Although she knew, in her heart, that she couldn't possibly be the best person for the job, she had agreed to care for an abandoned baby.

And she had also opened a door, of sorts, to Jake—
one she had intended to keep firmly shut.

Already she had remembered moments from the
past that would have been best left forgotten, happy
moments as well as sad. Moments when the way Jake
looked at her had made her pulse race.

But no more, Megan vowed. No matter what Alice
Radford or anyone else seemed to think. She had gotten herself into an untenable situation with her bra-
vado, and she had no choice but to see it through. On
her own, just as she'd always done, regardless of how
helpful Jake tried to be.

He hadn't been there for her when she needed him
after Will's death. She had no intention of counting
on him being there for her now. She had learned her
lesson well where he was concerned, and she wasn't
about to forget it anytime soon.

Chapter Four

Jake asked Darcy not to disturb him unless it was an emergency, then walked back to his office, shut the door, and closed the blinds on the window that looked out on the rest of the police station. The lavender scent of the soap Megan used lingered in the air along with the faint smell of baby powder, making it harder than it should have been for him to collect his thoughts.

When he sat back in his desk chair and closed his eyes, he could still see Megan sitting across from him, holding little Matthew in her arms. Hell, he could almost *feel* her there with him. And oddly enough, it was a feeling he was in no hurry to dispel.

Not once in all the months that Jake had been chief of police had he imagined Megan would come to see him at the station. That only a few minutes ago she had been tending to a baby right here in his office was almost more than he could believe. He hadn't anticipated just how unsettled he would be by the sight of his former wife holding a baby in her arms, either. Until then, he hadn't realized just how much he had lost, through his own fault.

Hearing that she had also completed the training necessary to serve as a foster parent had given him an additional jolt. He'd been reminded, none too gently, of how little he now knew about Megan's day-to-day activities, and that had saddened him deeply. They had always been so close, shared so much. Until she'd left him.

No, that wasn't true. Until *he* had left *her* alone to cope with their newborn son. That was when she had first drawn away from him, because *he* had drawn away from *her*. He had been the one to go off on one assignment, then another, as he'd always done, sure that Megan would manage on her own as she had always done.

She had managed, of course, just as she would with Matthew. But that fact didn't lessen the dismay Jake had felt ever since she'd agreed to care for the baby.

Mentally, he had cursed Alice Radford for even suggesting it. Megan's reluctance had been obvious to him, and understandable, yet the social worker hadn't seemed to notice. She had pressed Megan into service without the slightest hesitation, and Megan, bless her kind heart, hadn't seemed able to refuse.

Jake had no doubt at all about Megan's ability to care for Matthew. Despite the fear she'd voiced during her pregnancy that being orphaned at an early age might have left her lacking in maternal instincts, she had been a wonderful mother to Will. She would be equally devoted to Matthew, as well, and therein lay the real cause for his concern.

Jake had seen how attached Megan had become to the baby in the short time she'd already cared for him. The longer she was responsible for him, the more her bond with him would grow. Not a bad thing, at all, especially if it was determined that the baby truly had been abandoned. Megan, being his primary caregiver, would then be able to adopt him, as she probably would.

But if he did his job and found the baby's mother, as he was fairly sure he could do in a town the size of Serenity, Texas, then Megan could very well be devastated by the loss of another child—all thanks to *him.*

For the first time in his career as a law enforcement officer, Jake found himself faced with a dilemma to which he could see no favorable solution. He had hurt Megan so much already. And if he did as she asked, if he found Matthew's mother so she could be reunited with her infant son, Megan would be hurt again, possibly as much as she had been when Will died.

There wasn't anything Jake wanted to have happen less.

But Megan would know if he gave the search for Matthew's mother less than his best shot, and she wouldn't thank him for it. For the first time since she'd left him, she had come to him for help. He couldn't let her down, even in a no-win situation that promised heartache for her, as well for him.

What he could do, Jake acknowledged, was use his skills as an investigator to bring this particular case to a close just as soon as possible. The less time Megan spent with Matthew, the easier it would be for her to let him go. Which meant that he'd wasted enough time trying to sort out his own mixed emotions.

He had to get out on the street and start asking questions while the memory of a young woman pushing a baby stroller, either somewhere near the bus station or near Megan's house early that morning, would still be fresh in people's minds. Surely someone had seen something that would eventually lead him in the right direction.

With a sense of determination born of desperation, Jake pushed away from his desk, crossed his office and opened the door. To his relief, all was quiet in the station. One of the two young officers who had been there earlier had gone out on patrol as scheduled. The other sat at a desk using the hunt-and-peck method to type up a report on the annual end-of-school-year rash of senior pranks that thankfully had fallen far short of actual vandalism.

Darcy, too, seemed to be busy, apparently catching up on the filing. Jake had no doubt that once he left the station, she would have the telephone lines buzzing as she spread the word about the baby abandoned on Megan's front porch.

He could ask her to keep the information confidential, and she would. But what good would that do?

The dozen or more people around town who, by now, had more than likely seen Megan with the baby would have been talking about it for more than an hour already. Better to let Darcy put out the straight story so any wild rumors could be nipped in the bud right away.

Jake paused by the bank of filing cabinets, and Darcy glanced up at him expectantly.

"I'm going to see what I can find out about the woman who left her baby at Mrs. Cahill's house," he said. "I'll be heading over to the bus station first, then talking to people in her neighborhood. I'll have my cell phone with me in case you need me for anything."

"The woman who left the baby—was she young or old?" Darcy asked, her bright blue eyes sparkling with unabashed curiosity.

"Most likely young."

"Was Mrs. Cahill able to give you a description?"

"Vague at best. It was too dark for her to get a good look at her. But there's a chance someone else saw her and maybe recognized her. I trust you'll be talking to your friends about it. Let me know if you hear anything, okay?"

"I certainly will, Chief Cahill," Darcy assured him, her cheeks turning pink as she went back to her filing.

"Thanks, Darcy. See you later."

Jake never did get back to the police station that Friday. Once started on his search for Matthew's mother, he couldn't seem to stop, spurred on as he was by his desire to spare Megan as much heartache as possible. Unfortunately, he hit one dead end after another. Neither of the clerks at the bus station nor any of the people living on Megan's street remembered seeing a tall, slim young woman dressed in jeans, T-shirt and a baseball cap in the early morning hours, either with or without a baby in tow.

By early evening, Jake finally began to run out of steam. He would have to check back at the bus station later in case the woman had arrived during the late shift Thursday night. But he doubted that clerk would be any more interested in the comings and goings of the motor coach passengers than the two he had already questioned.

He would also have to have a couple of his men fan out along the other streets in Megan's neighborhood, asking questions, but that could wait until the following morning. It was almost six o'clock, he had put in a full day, and he just happened to be right outside Megan's house. He might as well stop by and let her know how the investigation was going, as he'd promised that morning.

She hadn't seemed pleased with the idea, but he wasn't going to let that stop him. He wanted to see her, and surprisingly, he wanted to see the baby, too. Not all of the memories of Will that little Matthew had stirred in him had been painful ones.

He wouldn't stay long, though. Especially if she seemed less than thrilled with his company. He didn't want to upset her any more than she probably was already.

As he climbed the steps to Megan's front porch,

Jake heard the sound of a baby crying through the door. His first instinct was to turn and walk away rather than intrude. The pitiful sound tugged at his heart, reminding him of all the times Will had made his own unhappiness known in exactly the same way. But the thought that Megan might be feeling rather frazzled after a day alone with a possibly cranky baby had him pressing a finger against the doorbell instead.

The door swung open after a few moments. Megan, clasping the wailing baby in her arms—and appearing to be just on the safe side of panicky—gazed at him, first with surprise, then with such obvious relief that Jake knew he'd made the right move.

"Thank goodness," she said, holding the baby out to him without the slightest hesitation. "Take Matthew for me, will you? I dropped the can of formula while I was trying to fill a bottle for him, and I've been having a devil of a time trying to open another one. I can't put him down because then he really starts to shriek, poor baby."

Jake took Matthew from her wordlessly, remembering with amazing ease how to position his hands to best support the baby's head and back. He was such a tiny mite, hardly weighing anything, so fragile and so vulnerable that Jake wanted only to cradle him close and keep him safe from all harm.

Matthew, his face red and damp with tears, stared at him through watery eyes for several seconds. Then he screwed up his tiny mouth and let out an outraged yowl, obviously not happy to be passed off to a stranger of the masculine persuasion. Feeling totally inadequate, Jake stepped into the house, shoved the door shut with one booted foot and followed Megan to the kitchen.

"Just a couple of minutes more," she advised, glancing over her shoulder at him as he paused uncertainly in the doorway. A pool of formula spread across the countertop and dripped down the front of a cabinet to spatter the tile floor, but she seemed much calmer as she warmed a bottle. "Why don't you sit at the table with him?"

Jake sat on one of the oak ladder-back chairs cushioned in a bright yellow flower print that matched the curtains at the window. He tried to soothe the baby with gentle pats on the back, but Matthew was having none of it. He was hungry and he wanted everyone within earshot to know it.

"Here you go." Megan came up beside his chair, holding out the bottle she'd prepared.

"Oh, hey, why don't you feed him?" Jake shifted in his chair and tried to hand the baby to her, sure that she could do a better job of it than he.

"I want to clean up the formula I spilled before the mess gets any worse," she said as she set the bottle on the table and turned away. Taking a dishcloth from one of the drawers and wetting it under the faucet, she added, "You remember how to give a baby a bottle, don't you?"

"Yes, of course," he muttered as he shifted Matthew from his shoulder to the crook of his arm and reluctantly reached for the bottle.

He could only hope that, like holding a baby, feeding one was a skill he'd learned for life.

As if aware that dinner was about to be served at

last, the baby stopped crying, waved his arms excitedly and made little smacking sounds with his mouth.

"Hungry, are you?" Jake asked, smiling in spite of being nervous as Matthew latched onto the nipple and started to suck.

He remembered Megan showing him how to tilt the bottle with Will so he wouldn't gulp down air bubbles along with the formula, and did the same with Matthew. Whether consciously or not, the baby put his tiny hand on Jake's as he held the bottle. His smile deepening, Jake took the gesture as a sign of approval and relaxed considerably. He was doing okay with the baby, and he felt damn good about it.

"Thanks, Jake." Megan glanced at him gratefully, then finished wiping down the cabinet. "Your timing couldn't have been any better. I was just about ready to lose it. I'd forgotten how hard it could be taking care of a baby, single-handed."

"Hey, no problem. I'm glad I could help out," Jake assured her.

"I was actually doing okay until the can of formula got away from me..."

Her words trailing off, Megan rinsed the dishcloth in the sink, then stooped down to mop up the puddle on the floor.

His attention caught by the slightly defensive edge he heard in Megan's voice, Jake shifted his gaze to her. There was a rigid set to her shoulders as she scrubbed at the floor. Obviously, she had doubts about her ability to care for Matthew on her own, and that surprised him, considering how often she had coped on her own with Will.

"I'm sure you were doing just fine," he said, offering her the reassurance she seemed to need.

"Well, I'm not," she muttered as she stood to rinse out the dishcloth again.

"You did just fine with Will all those times I was away," he reminded her, then realized, too late, that he'd opened a door on the past she probably would have preferred to leave closed.

But he'd been doing what she preferred for almost a year now. How could talking about the past, about *Will,* be any worse then continuing to act as if nothing had happened?

Slowly Megan turned to look at him, her pale gray eyes flashing angrily.

"No, I didn't do *just fine* with Will all those times you were away. I did the best I could because I didn't have any other choice."

"But you never said anything," he protested, his own defenses going up.

She had never once complained of feeling inadequate. Nor had she ever seemed overwhelmed by the responsibilities of motherhood. How was he supposed to have known?

"What could I have said, Jake? Please don't get involved in another high-profile undercover case that will take you away for weeks at a time. Stay home with me instead, and help me take care of our baby. Would you have asked to be reassigned to office duty for even six months? Would you, Jake, honestly and truthfully?" She turned her back on him again and shut off the faucet with a snap of her wrist, adding quietly, "I didn't think so, so I didn't ask."

She was right, of course. He had been too damn involved in climbing the bureau's ladder to consider taking time away from his undercover work. But maybe if she'd let him know how she had been feeling, he could have made some compromises on her behalf. Maybe if she'd told him what a hard time she sometimes had with the baby instead of soldiering on in silence he would have made an effort to be there for her more often. Then again, maybe he wouldn't have.

"I'm not sure what I would have done," he admitted, answering her with the honesty she'd demanded of him. "I can only say what I wish I'd done, and that's be home with you and Will a hell of a lot more than I was." He paused, looking down at Matthew, and thought of all the evenings he could have spent sitting at the table, giving the baby a bottle, while Megan puttered around the kitchen. "I missed so much, being gone the way I was."

"Well, you know what they say about hindsight being twenty-twenty," Megan replied, her tone once again cool and matter-of-fact.

Oh, yes, Jake thought, he knew all too well about that. Had he had any clue about what the future would bring, he would have never put his job before his wife and child. Instead, he had taken for granted that they would always be there waiting for him, grateful for whatever scraps of time he managed to throw their way. He had never considered how quickly he could lose them, one after another, until they both were gone.

"I've made so many mistakes," he acknowledged regretfully.

"We both have," Megan said, her tone clipped. "No sense going over and over it, though. What's done is done. There's no going back and changing it."

Jake knew that, too. What he had a hard time accepting was that they couldn't learn—together—from those mistakes, and become a couple again.

He thought about saying as much to Megan, but after a quick glance at her, he decided not to. She had a brook-no-argument look about her that warned he'd be wasting his breath. He remembered all too well how resistant she could be when her mouth narrowed into a thin line.

She had already relented more in the past few minutes than she had in the past twelve months, listening to at least some of what he wanted to say to her. He didn't want her shutting him out again because he'd pushed her too hard, too fast.

Focusing on the baby, Jake saw that Matthew's eyes were now at half-mast. He sucked down the last of the formula, then let the nipple slide out of his mouth.

"All finished, little boy?" he asked as he set the empty bottle on the table.

"I can take him now," Megan said, tossing a clean cloth diaper over her shoulder as she came up beside him again.

Suddenly as reluctant to hand over the baby as he'd been only a short while ago to give him the bottle, Jake met Megan's gaze.

"I don't mind burping him," he advised, smiling slightly. "I remember how to do that, too."

"All right." Her fingers brushing against his, Megan handed him the cloth diaper. Then, as if burned by his touch, she pulled her hand away, quickly turned and crossed to the refrigerator. "Are you hungry?" she asked, opening the door with a jerky movement. "I could make sandwiches."

Jake eyed her with surprise, wondering if he'd heard her right. She had her back to him as she rummaged around in the refrigerator, so he couldn't see the expression on her face. But her tone, while less than inviting, had been conciliatory, and that was good enough for him. He wasn't going to give up any opportunity to be with her if he could help it.

"Sounds good to me," he said. "I missed lunch."

"Ham and cheese okay?"

"Yeah, sure."

She set packages of each on the counter along with a jar of mustard, then took a fresh loaf of bread from the bread box and plates from one of the cabinets.

"Have you found out anything about Matthew's mother?" she asked as she spread mustard onto two slices of the bread.

Obviously, she wanted to shift their conversation onto more neutral ground. Jake had no problem with that.

"Not yet," he replied. "I've questioned two of the clerks at the bus station, along with the owners of the businesses nearby. I've also gone door-to-door on your street without any luck. Nobody seems to have seen a young woman fitting our description, either with or without a baby in a stroller, at the bus station or anywhere near your house. Half a dozen people, however, do remember seeing *you* with the baby later in the morning."

"Well, of course," Megan acknowledged, glancing over at him with a wry smile.

Jake smiled, too, warmed by the fact that she was relaxing with him just a bit.

"I'm going to talk to the night clerk when he comes on duty later this evening, and I'm going to have a couple of my officers talk to the people living on the streets within a three-mile radius of your house tomorrow. So far, though, Matthew's mother's identity is still a mystery. That's the main reason why I stopped by here. I thought you'd want to know how the investigation's going."

"Yes, thanks. I did." Megan looked noticeably relieved as she set the plates with their sandwiches on the table. "I have iced tea and soft drinks," she offered.

"Tea would be good."

Jake continued to gently pat Matthew's back though the baby had already burped satisfactorily. Megan's reaction to his news, while exactly what he'd expected it to be, also caused him some concern. She had asked him to find Matthew's mother, but he had a feeling that deep in her heart, she hoped he wouldn't succeed.

"Looks like he's asleep," Megan said as she returned to the table with two glasses of tea. "I'd better put him to bed."

She reached out to take Matthew from him, but

Jake wasn't ready to relinquish the baby just yet. Tending to the abandoned infant had put him more in touch with his own feelings, and with Megan, than he had been in longer than he could remember.

Since first taking Matthew from her, he'd been inundated with memories, more happy than sad. Until then, he had avoided thinking about the past in any great detail because he'd believed it would be too painful. But there, in Megan's kitchen, doing something as simple as giving the baby a bottle, he had experienced a long-forgotten sense of peace and contentment that he wanted to hang on to as long as he possibly could.

"I can take him up," he said as he stood. "Just show me the way."

Megan hesitated, a frown furrowing her forehead as she avoided his gaze. Then, with a negligent shrug, she turned on her heel abruptly.

"If you insist," she said, walking out of the kitchen ahead of him.

Jake grimaced at her off-putting tone as he followed her across the living room. Two steps forward, then one step back, he thought to himself. Not exactly the progress he would have liked to be making with her, but better than no progress at all.

Though he had to walk fast to keep up with Megan, Jake managed to glimpse enough of the living room to realize that it was rather sparsely and impersonally furnished. Her good taste showed in the comfortable-looking sofa and armchair, the dark wood end tables and brass lamps, and the matching armoire that held a television set and a small stereo system. But there weren't any photographs on display, any pictures on the walls or plants in the windows.

No one would know, by looking around, that she had lived in the house for two years, and that saddened him greatly. Megan had made their home together a warm and vibrant place to be, adding all sorts of special touches that were missing here. This might be the house where she lived, but she seemed to have allowed herself no real attachment to it.

"The baby's room is in here," she said, gesturing to an open doorway off to the left as he reached the top of the stairs.

Enough daylight still peeped through the slats of the blinds on the window to guide his way into the nursery. A crib made up with pale blue sheets and a fluffy blanket stood against one wall. There was also a small chest of drawers and changing table stacked with disposable diapers, a container of wet wipes, baby powder and lotion.

"Is a diaper change in order?" Jake asked, pausing just inside the room. It, too, lacked the personal touches Megan had added to Will's nursery, most noticeably the pile of stuffed animals she had bought to keep their baby company.

"I changed him right before you got here," Megan replied as she moved past him to turn back the blanket on the crib. "He should be okay for now."

Moving across the room, Jake gently shifted Matthew from his shoulder, then laid the sleeping baby in the crib. Matthew's eyes fluttered delicately, but he didn't awake. With a tiny baby sigh, he raised one little thumb to his rosebud mouth and began to suck contentedly.

"Pacifier?" Jake asked, smiling as he glanced at Megan.

"No, he seems to prefer his thumb." She met his gaze, also smiling, seemingly caught, as he was, in the same tender moment of remembering that Will, too, had preferred his thumb to a pacifier.

He thought that she would withdraw again as she'd done each time she realized that she'd lowered her guard. But she continued to look at him, her pale gray eyes filled with a longing that reached into him and touched his soul.

Not stopping to consider how she would respond, Jake reached out for her. Hands on her shoulders, he pulled her close, bent his head and kissed her.

She tensed for a moment. Then she relaxed against him with a sigh much like Matthew's, angling her head, allowing him to deepen their kiss in a way that made his heart, and his hopes, soar anew.

Chapter Five

*S*top, Megan ordered herself. *Stop acting like a love-starved fool, and stop, stop, stop kissing Jake.*

But it feels so good, another part of her chimed in as she clung to him, her hands gripping the crisp fabric of his cotton shirt. *He* felt so good—so warm, so familiar and so very, very enticing….

His hands moved over her without the slightest bit of hesitation, down her back to her hips and then her buttocks, lifting her against him, revealing the true depth of his desire.

As if she'd been doused with a bucket of icy water, Megan pulled away from him. Breathing hard, hands clenched at her sides, she refused to look at him as she took a long step back.

What on earth had come over her, not to mention

Jake? How dare he take advantage of her jumbled emotions and use them against her?

"You'd better go," she said, making no effort whatsoever to hide her anger.

"Megan, please," he murmured, reaching out to touch her cheek. "I only wanted to—"

"I don't care *what* you wanted, although you made it pretty obvious," she shot back as she knocked his hand away. Turning her back on him, she added brusquely, "Just go, Jake. Please, just go."

For one long moment, Megan thought he would refuse. Finally, though, he moved past her to the bedroom doorway. There he paused.

"I'll be in touch if I find out anything about Matthew's mother," he said, his voice surprisingly calm.

With barely a blink of an eye, he had once again taken on the role of Serenity's chief of police. Megan knew she should be grateful. He was going along with what she wanted, after all.

She would never have kissed him if he hadn't caught her in a moment of weakness. Memories of all the joy they'd once shared had undermined her defenses. And that wouldn't have happened if she hadn't let him into her house in the first place.

"Just give me a call," she said, fussing with Matthew's blanket so she wouldn't have to look at Jake again.

"Stopping by is no problem. That way I can lend a hand with Matthew again."

Megan couldn't think of anything she wanted Jake to do less, but by the time she whipped around to tell him so, he'd left the bedroom. She could run after him, of course, and tell him to stay away. Instead, she stood where she was, listening as he let himself out of her house. The hollow click of the front door closing echoed all around her.

She had been so glad to see him earlier, standing on her front porch—too glad for her own good, she realized now. But she had been in a bit of a bind at the time, and having his help with the baby had made all the difference to her state of mind.

She had forgotten how hard it sometimes was to care for an infant all on your own, and she had been very close to panicking. With Jake there, speaking a few words of encouragement in a soothing voice as he lent a helping hand, the tilt had gone out of her temporarily rattled world.

It was amazing, and utterly annoying, Megan thought. Especially considering that she'd been so grateful she had lowered her guard enough for him to think kissing her was all right.

She didn't want to be beholden to Jake, not under any circumstances, and certainly not to the point where she fell into his arms like a silly fool. She had managed to get by without him for the past two years. She would just as soon continue in the same vein, no matter how her heart fluttered at the memory of his tongue sweeping over hers.

Pressing her fingertips to her slightly swollen lips, Megan gave herself a firm mental shake. She had Matthew's best interests to consider, as well as her own, and she couldn't find his mother by herself. She needed Jake's help for that. And tonight, whether she'd liked it or not, his help with the baby had also come in very handy.

Looking back on the time they had spent together in her kitchen, she couldn't believe how casually she'd behaved. Of course, her first priority had been fixing a bottle for Matthew as quickly as she possibly could. She had been too preoccupied to hide behind the facade of indifference she always assumed whenever Jake entered her orbit.

As for Jake...

Although he'd seemed just a bit flustered at first, he had handled the baby in his own easygoing way. Granted, she hadn't given him much of a choice, but he *had* been a good sport. And between the two of them they had gotten the baby fed and the kitchen cleaned up just as they had those times when he had been home with her and Will. Those all-too-rare times, as he had finally admitted.

Too bad he hadn't realized what he was missing until it was too late, Megan thought, smoothing a hand over Matthew's downy head—too bad for all of them.

With a barely audible sigh, she moved away from the crib at last, paused to turn on the night-light on the dresser, then headed back downstairs. She wasn't sure how long he would sleep. He might want another bottle at ten o'clock, then sleep until early morning, or he might sleep until two or three, then be ready to eat again. One way or another, he would let her know what kind of schedule he was on.

In the meantime, she might as well prepare several bottles of formula and store them in the refrigerator.

Then she wouldn't have a repeat of this evening's unfortunate incident. The one thing she had forgotten about those first weeks of motherhood was the importance of taking advantage of whatever spare moments she had. With Will, she had learned to eat, sleep and take a shower at the oddest times of day or night. It had been either that or do without.

In the kitchen, the sandwiches and iced tea Megan had set out for Jake and herself still sat on the table, untouched. Her offer of a meal had been a big mistake, she thought as she dumped one glass of tea down the drain, then wrapped one sandwich in waxed paper.

She had made it seem like she wanted him to stay when she shouldn't have. The only thing she'd had to gain by letting him hang around her house any longer than absolutely necessary was more aggravation. And that's exactly what she'd gotten upstairs in the nursery.

Cursing her vulnerability to Jake yet again, Megan sat at the table and reached for her sandwich. Though she wasn't especially hungry, she knew she'd better eat while she had a moment's peace. And she'd be wise to think of something besides Jake's kiss, as well.

Impossible on both counts, she admitted after only a few seconds, setting aside her sandwich. Jake's presence in her cozy kitchen, even for such a short time, had left an indelible mark. Having felt the force of his masculinity, she was all the more aware of its absence now. It had been one thing to imagine him in her home, as she had secretly done more times than she cared to admit. It was something else altogether to have actually experienced it.

Taking a sip of her tea, Megan reminded herself sternly that her home, like her life, had been just fine minus Jake Cahill, and would continue to be if only she'd stop being fanciful. Kiss or no kiss, he had only come there on official business. She had been the one to upset the delicate balance between them when she asked for his help. She couldn't blame him completely for using the opening she'd given him to his advantage. But she could make sure it didn't happen again.

She didn't want him to think there was a chance they could get back together again. Especially when it seemed that he was considering Bobby Fuentes's request that he return to the bureau.

In the early days of their marriage, Megan hadn't minded the undercover work that had taken Jake away, sometimes for weeks at a time. She had taught full-time during the school year, and summers she'd taken a class or two toward her master's degree. She'd also had friends of her own, so she'd never had any trouble keeping busy. When Jake came home, more often than not triumphant at having closed another case, their time together had been very special, not to mention very intense.

All that had changed after Will was born, though. Megan had quit her job to stay home with the baby, a luxury she had initially been glad they could afford. Unfortunately, she had also seen less and less of her friends, none of whom had children yet. As for honeymoon reunions with Jake…

More often than not, she had been too exhausted by the demands of twenty-four-hour-a-day, seven-day-a-week child care—occasionally even too angry—to do more than give him a begrudging peck on the cheek. *His* life hadn't really changed except for the times when he was at home. And those times had grown less and less frequent as her welcome became cooler and more distant.

Neither one of them had been prepared for the upheaval the baby had brought to the life they shared. And neither one of them had thought to ask for help in dealing with that upheaval. They had drawn away from each other rather than together during those ten months after Will's birth. And when he died, the badly frayed bonds of their marriage had ripped apart completely.

Instead of turning to each other in the face of tragedy as they once would have done, they had grown even more distant. Jake had thrown himself into his work, leaving Megan to grieve alone, and eventually, telling herself she had nothing left to lose, she had moved back to Serenity.

Megan hadn't expected Jake to follow her there. More than that, she hadn't *wanted* him to. The day he'd come to see her, her defenses had gone up automatically, and had stayed up ever since.

Recalling how she'd behaved, she wondered if she'd been too harsh toward him, too unforgiving. He hadn't been responsible for Will's death, after all. *She* was more to blame for that. She had been too unsure of what to do, too hesitant to question the pediatrician, too slow to take the baby to the emergency room.

But if Jake had been home that fateful night maybe they could have made the right decisions together—decisions that would have saved their son's life. She had trusted that he would be there for her when she really needed him, and the one and only time she had, he'd let her down. Then he had come to Serenity, in his own good time, thinking he could regain her trust.

No way, Megan thought, as she had almost a year ago. No way would she ever allow herself to trust Jake again—not personally. And without trust, what else could she have with him?

Unbidden, the memory of his kiss came to her yet again, along with a wave of longing so intense that her breath caught in her throat. She could tell herself that she wanted nothing more to do with Jake, but she knew she was lying.

She hadn't kept her distance from him all these months just to be ornery. She had stayed away from him because she had never really gotten over him, and she knew in her heart there was a good chance she never would.

The chime of the front doorbell drew Megan from her reverie. Considering the trail her thoughts had been taking, she half hoped, half dreaded that Jake had returned. Pushing away from the table, she headed for the living room, her heart pounding.

Instead of Jake, Megan found Margaret Griffin, her friend Emma's mother-in-law, standing on her front porch.

"I heard you had some excitement here today,"

Margaret said. Smiling, she held out a foil-covered casserole dish from which a mouth-watering aroma wafted. "I thought maybe you might not have had time to fix dinner."

"I was just eating a sandwich." Returning Margaret's smile, Megan took the dish from her, then tipped her head in an inviting nod. "Would you like to come in?"

"Are you sure you're up to more company?" Margaret asked as she stepped into the house and closed the door.

"More company?" Megan eyed her curiously.

"I drove by earlier and saw that Jake was here."

"He stopped by to tell me he hadn't found out anything about the baby's mother yet."

Wondering if Margaret knew that Jake had been there much longer than it would have taken to relay such information, Megan turned to lead the way to the kitchen, a blush warming her cheeks.

"So it *is* true someone left a baby on your doorstep early this morning, and Alice Radford talked you into fostering him temporarily."

"Yes, very true," Megan admitted. "Would you like some tea?"

"That would be lovely, dear."

Megan put the casserole dish in the refrigerator, then poured a glass of tea for Margaret, explaining all the while how she'd found Matthew in his stroller, gone to Jake to ask for his help in locating the baby's mother, and ended up home again with Matthew consigned to her care.

"Nothing like leaping into the county foster care program with both feet," Margaret said.

"I didn't have much choice. Alice was really short-handed," Megan admitted ruefully.

"You'll do just fine, dear," Margaret assured her. "And I'll be happy to help out any way I can. I'm an experienced granny, you know, but with Sam and Emma living in Colorado Springs my grandchildren are too far away to spoil as much as I'd like. You would be doing me a great favor letting me keep my hand in with Matthew."

"Put that way, I don't see how I can refuse."

Megan smiled gratefully, aware of how much having someone like Margaret Griffin close by would have helped after Will's birth. Her parents and Jake's mother had all passed away by then, though, and Jake's father, Senator William Cahill, had been busy politicking in Austin.

"I'm sure Jake would be happy to lend a hand, too," Margaret added as Megan joined her at the table.

"He's doing more than enough already, looking for the baby's mother," Megan hedged, avoiding Margaret's steady gaze.

Emma's mother-in-law had been a good friend to her, looking out for her since she'd returned to Serenity, more than likely at Emma's behest. Megan appreciated Margaret's kindness and concern, and made a point of returning the favor on a regular basis, as much out of genuine liking for the older woman as to help ease Emma's mind. But she didn't feel any more willing to take advice from her about Jake as she had from Alice Radford.

"He'll do an excellent job of it, to be sure. But spending time with the baby would also be good for him. As good as it will be for you. Caring for an infant reminds us of how precious a new life is. And it helps ease the pain of the losses we've suffered by making us realize how much of ourselves we still have to give."

Megan couldn't argue with Margaret. In the short time Matthew had been in her care, the aching emptiness left inside of her by Will's death had finally begun to ease. She had seen, too, Jake's tenderness toward the baby, and realized now that his spirit had to have been renewed, as well.

"I wouldn't want to impose on him," she said, still equivocating. "He's the chief of police—"

"Of a relatively small, quiet town," Margaret pointed out in a humorous tone. "I doubt he'd ever be too busy to lend you a helping hand."

"He was after Will was born," Megan stated, her voice quavering slightly as she finally met her friend's gaze.

"More than likely because he didn't know better then. I'd wager he's changed a lot in the time that's passed."

"So have I."

"Yes, of course. But not so much that you don't care about each other anymore. Anyone with eyes in their head can see that. Give him another chance, Megan, and give yourself another chance, too."

"I wish I could," Megan replied, looking away

again. Then, anxious to change the subject, she asked about Emma and Sam.

Margaret hesitated only a moment, then filled Megan in on the latest news she'd had from her son and daughter-in-law as Megan bit into her sandwich. Megan was glad to hear they were planning a visit later in the summer. She was also glad that the older woman said nothing more about Jake.

"Well, dear, I'd better head home and let you enjoy the peace and quiet while you can," Margaret finished, smiling as she stood.

"Would you like to see the baby first?" Megan asked, as eager to show off her young charge as if he were her own child.

"I'd like that very much, although I wouldn't want to risk waking him."

"He seems to be a pretty sound sleeper, but I'm not sure what kind of schedule he's on yet. He might actually be ready to wake up on his own."

Margaret followed Megan upstairs to the makeshift nursery, and together they admired Matthew as he slept in his crib, seeming not the least bit disturbed by their presence.

"He's a beautiful baby," Margaret commented after they had gone downstairs again. "I can't imagine how his mother could have given him up. Unless she's in some kind of trouble...."

"That was my thought, too," Megan admitted. "I'm just hoping Jake can find her, and we can help her resolve whatever difficulties she's having so she can have him back again."

"But then you'll have to give him up." Margaret

frowned, her concern evident as she paused on the front porch.

"Well, yes, but if his mother loves him as much as I have a feeling she does, I won't mind," Megan replied, saying aloud what she so desperately needed to believe.

Reuniting Matthew with his mother was the best way this particular situation could end, even if it hurt her personally to give him up. She knew better than to become too attached to him—knew it in her head, but in her heart...

"You'll call me if you need anything—anything at all?" Margaret asked.

"Yes, I will. And thanks, again, for the casserole."

To Megan's relief, Matthew awoke about ten o'clock, ready for a diaper change and another bottle, then slept through the night, awakening again just after six Saturday morning.

By the time she had him fed, bathed and dressed in a fresh romper, and had showered and dressed in yellow shorts and a sleeveless, yellow-and-white striped shirt herself, the morning was half gone, though. And then, to her surprise, and mild dismay, there began an unexpected parade of well-meaning visitors, all curious about the new addition to her family, and all offering to help out in any way they could—much as Margaret Griffin had.

Her nearest neighbors stopped by with salads, casseroles and homemade cakes, as did several of her fellow teachers at the high school. Even Steven Barns, the principal, came bearing a pan of his spinach la-

sagna. And he seemed delighted to hold Matthew during one of his fussier moments, despite the glob of
spit-up that landed on his pale blue knit shirt.

Considering how she had kept to herself since
she'd returned to Serenity, Megan was amazed at how
many people seemed to care about her. Granted, they
were also interested in the baby she'd found on her
front porch, but in a kindly way. And, as she'd done
when Margaret offered her help the night before, Megan realized how different her life as a new mother
might have been had she and Jake lived in Serenity
when Will was born.

She would have had friends and neighbors of all
ages offering to lend a hand from the day their baby
was born because that was what folks in a town like
Serenity, Texas, did.

Megan was most surprised by the midafternoon arrival of three of her former students from her first year
of teaching at Serenity High School. All three had
been top students, and although they had each gone
to different universities, they had apparently remained
good friends.

Amanda Lawler, home for the summer from Stan-
ford, still favored gauzy skirts, peasant blouses and
sandals, and still wore her long, light brown hair in a
braid. Christina Evans, home from Sarah Lawrence,
had shorn her auburn hair rather severely, but still
looked ready for a meeting of the Junior League in
her beige linen pants and sleeveless, black silk shirt.
And Jilly Maitland, home from Northwestern, her
pale, shoulder-length blond hair swinging softly to her

shoulders, looked as fit and trim as ever in denim shorts and a red tank top.

They chattered excitedly about the baby, napping in the nursery, quieting only long enough to take a quick peak at him, each fresh young face softening perceptibly. Then, downstairs again, they sampled some of the food Megan offered while filling her in on their various experiences away at school.

Jilly, Megan's favorite of the three, seemed slightly more reserved than the others, but then, she always had been, Megan remembered.

The young women stayed until Matthew awoke from his nap. They passed him around gently, delighting in his sweet smiles while Megan warmed a bottle for him. Then, with cheery waves and promises to visit again, they let themselves out as she settled down to feed the baby.

In the sudden silence, Megan cuddled Matthew close. Much as she had enjoyed the company of her neighbors, fellow teachers and former students, she was content to have the baby all to herself again.

Remembering the way Steven Barns had juggled Matthew while trying hard to ignore the regurgitated formula on his shirt had her smiling all over again. And her mouth watered at the thought of the plate of brownies left by Mrs. Bukowski, her neighbor from across the street, along with the spray of fresh-cut roses from her husband's garden scenting the living room air.

She began to make a mental list of the other visitors she'd had so she could send each a note of appreciation, then caught herself musing that the one person she expected to see that day hadn't come to the house at all.

There was still time for Jake to stop by, of course, but somehow Megan didn't think he would. Not unless he had something to report on the baby's missing mother from the day's investigation, which had surely ended by now.

With all the people who *had* come to see her, Megan knew she shouldn't mind Jake's absence, at least not as much as she did. She had taken on the job of caring for Matthew, not him, and she certainly didn't need his help with it. *His* job was to find the baby's mother—a job that didn't require him to spend time with her.

But he had stopped by yesterday evening, and despite her earlier attempts to convince herself otherwise, she had liked having him in her house. Just as she'd liked the kiss they'd shared enough to hope he would come to see her again today.

Foolishly, of course, but where Jake Cahill was concerned, she'd often had trouble sorting her fantasies from reality. She had assumed that after two years apart, she'd gotten better at it. Apparently, she had assumed wrong. She could, and would, continue to work on it, though.

"Just as soon as I have a brownie," she told Matthew as he gazed up at her with his big blue eyes.

A year ago, Megan hadn't wanted to even try to reconcile with Jake, and she'd had valid reasons for making that decision. She *still* had valid reasons. There was nothing wrong with needing his help to find Matthew's mother. Letting her need for him grow into something more personal—something that spoke of intimate expectations—had to be avoided, though.

She had suffered her fair share of disappointment at his hands. She wasn't about to set herself up for more of the same.

Chapter Six

Jake hadn't had an easy time staying away from Megan's house on Saturday. He could have justified being the last of the steady stream of visitors she'd had since midmorning. Neither he nor any of his officers had turned up a lead on the baby's mother. But that fact, in and of itself, would have given him reason enough to go knocking at his former wife's door.

Driving by her house an embarrassing number of times, he had argued the pros and cons of it until his head ached. In the end, however, he had headed back to his father's rambling old ranch house on the outskirts of town after he clocked out for the day, and for the most ridiculous of reasons.

Jake had chosen not to see Megan on Saturday evening simply because he would have found it too hard to leave her again once he'd filled her in on the status of his investigation.

He'd known better than to think she would invite him into her home again so soon. Not after the way he had behaved the previous night. Her emotions might have been stirred by his kiss—hell, no *might* have about it. She had kissed him back with a passion too obvious for either of them to deny. But she'd been angered, as well, not only by his sensual advances, but also by her own eager, unguarded response.

In those moments when she had melted against him, opening her mouth to taste and be tasted in a delightfully familiar way, Jake had seen the future shift and change as he had almost given up believing it would. And he certainly hadn't thought all was lost just because she had sent him packing.

Granted, her defenses had been firmly in place again, but he'd carved a chink in the wall she'd built around her heart. He didn't want to risk having her seal it tight again because he was pushing her too hard, too fast. Better to give her a little time to adjust to the idea of having him in her life again.

Just a little time, though. They had finally begun to talk about the past—tentatively, at least. He wasn't about to lose what momentum he had built up in that direction. Nor was he going to give up the opportunity to spend time with her and Matthew while the baby was in her care.

As he had tended to the abandoned infant last night, Jake had been reminded all too painfully of the losses he'd brought upon himself. But he had also realized that life went on, and as it did, one was given a chance to right wrongs, to adjust attitudes, to understand, at last, what was really important in life. Little things like sitting at a kitchen table, giving a baby a bottle while the woman you loved hovered close by.

Still, he had decided not to see Megan Saturday night. All he had to tell her—straight away—was that his search for Matthew's mother continued to be unsuccessful. And having to stand on her front porch, literally hat in hand to do so, would have been too humiliating for him to bear.

He could have called her, of course, and given her the necessary information over the telephone. In fact, he'd thought about it when he arrived at his father's house. But he'd put it off until he'd taken a shower and dressed in shorts and a T-shirt, then had a beer, and another. Until he'd finally told himself it was too late to risk waking the baby.

By early Sunday afternoon, however, Jake finally managed to convince himself that he was not only duty-bound to pay a visit to his ex-wife, but he'd also waited long enough to do it. He had a no-progress report to make, he had the day off, and truth be told, there wasn't anything else he'd rather do. Maybe by the time he got to her house, he'd not only be able to think of a way to get past her front door; he would have also thought of a reason to hang around for a while, too.

As he pulled up in front of Megan's house, Jake saw a small, moderately sporty, dark green car already parked at the curb. He didn't recognize it as belonging to anyone he knew around town, but he remembered seeing the same car there the previous afternoon when he'd made one of his passes by the house.

He thought about driving on, postponing his own visit for an hour or two so he wouldn't have to compete with someone else for Megan's attention. But he was curious about the person who had made an effort to stop by Megan's house two days in a row.

At least it wasn't Steven Barns, Jake thought as he pulled into the driveway. Unless old Barns had traded in his modest sedan for something a bit snazzier...

Jake ambled up to the porch with a surface nonchalance that belied his inner agitation. Contrary to what he'd hoped as he'd set off to see Megan, he hadn't come up with a good reason to get inside the front door, much less stay there for any amount of time should he get so lucky. He could just *ask* if he could come in. He doubted she'd refuse, but such a move on his part would surely make her wary.

With an exasperated sigh, Jake pressed the doorbell, then rocked back on his heels as the chimes echoed through the house. Several minutes passed, and Megan didn't come to the door, so he rang the bell again, then slowly counted to ten as he continued to wait.

"Jake? Hello..."

Megan's voice came from behind him, causing him to whirl around in surprise. She stood at the base of the porch steps, looking up at him from under the wide brim of a floppy straw hat. She was dressed in ratty denim cutoff shorts and a faded red tank top that had obviously seen better days, and she held a pair of gardening gloves in one hand.

Despite the smudges of dirt on her arms and legs, she looked absolutely gorgeous to him. Of course, he had always been partial to the way knit shirts clung to her breasts and shorts showed off her long, trim legs.

She smiled slightly, adding, "I was in the backyard weeding the rose bed by the gazebo, and I thought I heard the doorbell ring."

Jake hesitated a moment, her unexpected welcome tilting his world. Then, drawing a steadying breath, he crossed to the top of the porch steps, paused and shoved his hands in the back pockets of his khaki shorts.

"I just stopped by to let you know how the investigation's going. Do you have a few minutes to talk?"

"Sure." She gestured for him to join her as she turned to follow the stone pathway that led around the side of the house. "Come on back to the gazebo. I was just about to stop for a glass of iced tea. Would you like one, too?"

"Sounds good to me," he readily agreed, determined to sip it as slowly as he could.

Maybe he'd even work up the nerve to ask about the sandwich he'd left behind Friday night…teasingly, of course.

"How about you, Jilly? Would you like a glass of iced tea?" Megan asked as she led the way into the backyard.

"Yes, thanks. That would be lovely."

Pausing again just inside the wooden fence that afforded Megan's yard the intimate privacy of an old-fashioned cottage garden, Jake eyed the young woman sitting on a faded patchwork quilt spread under the shady branches of a huge, sprawling oak tree. Half turned away from him, she had her attention focused on the baby sleeping beside her on the quilt.

Even before she swept a hand through her shoulder-length blond hair and glanced his way, he could see that she was quite pretty. She also looked vaguely familiar, but he couldn't put a name to her face. He did note, however, that she seemed somewhat taken aback by his arrival.

"Jake, have you met Jilly Maitland?" Megan asked. "Her parents live in your father's neighborhood. Her father is chief of staff at the hospital. And Jilly, this is Jake Cahill, Serenity's chief of police."

"Hello, Jilly," Jake said, smiling as he nodded an acknowledgement, his memory jogged by the mention of her surname. "We met years ago at a country club get-together, but I was closer to your age then and you were still a toddler. We're lucky to have a man like your father running our hospital."

"Thank you, Chief Cahill," Jilly replied, blushing as she looked away.

"Jilly attends Northwestern University in Chicago," Megan added as she opened the backdoor. "She was also one of my best students at Serenity High School. She stopped by yesterday with a couple of friends. We didn't have much of a chance to talk, though, so she decided to come back again today. She's been keeping an eye on Matthew for me while I do battle with the weeds in the rose garden. Margaret Griffin mentioned that Emma is going to be in town at the end of July, and the garden was her pride and joy. I don't want her thinking I've been neglect-ful.''

"The roses are beautiful, Mrs. Cahill," Jilly assured her, then glanced at her watch and scrambled to her feet. "Gosh, look at the time. I have to get home. My parents are taking me to the country club for a welcome home dinner, and I really should wash my hair. I'm glad I got to meet you, Chief Cahill. Bye, Mrs. Cahill.''

"Bye, Jilly." A bemused expression on her face, Megan watched as Jilly walked quickly toward the gate.

Frowning thoughtfully, Jake also watched Jilly hurry away. She had seemed perfectly content to stay for a glass of tea until she'd seen him. Why had she changed her mind so abruptly? She didn't seem like the type to be intimidated by his position. He wasn't even in uniform. Growing up a Maitland certainly would have given her the necessary poise to handle almost any situation, as well.

"I hope she didn't feel like she had to leave on my account," he said after a moment. "I didn't mean to interrupt anything important.''

"Just girl talk," Megan assured him. "We can pick up where we left off another day. She'll be home all summer. Will you keep an eye on Matthew while I get the tea?''

"Sure.''

As Megan stepped inside the house, Jake took Jilly's place on the quilt, hunkering down beside the sleeping baby. Thoughts of the young woman quickly left his mind as he focused on little Matthew. Tracing a finger along the curve of his cheek, Jake realized again, as he had Friday night, just how innocent, how fragile and how vulnerable an infant was.

Without the care and protection of at least one loving parent, untold harm could come to him. How lucky for Will that Megan had been willing to fill the gaps *he* had left by his increasing absence. And how lucky for Matthew that she was willing to take over for the mother who had so recklessly abandoned him.

He would gladly help her, if she'd let him, Jake mused. He no longer had the kind of job that took him away for long periods of time. But neither did he have Megan's love and trust.

She might have weakened toward him enough to kiss him back Friday evening, but then she'd immediately sent him on his way. And while she hadn't seemed angry or upset to see him standing on her front porch a few minutes ago, neither had she seemed especially pleased. While she might have accepted their mutual interest in Matthew's welfare, she saw their roles as separate. She'd made that clear the other night. But maybe he could convince her otherwise, not so much with words as with actions.

Though it was warm out, the gentle breeze drifting through the branches of the oak tree was cool and refreshing. In another month or so, the air would be heating up with humidity, making even shady spots uncomfortable in the afternoon. But today the weather was almost perfect. And there was a kind of peacefulness about Megan's backyard that eased the tension from his body.

Shifting his gaze to the little lattice-work gazebo,

its interior mysteriously shadowed, Jake listened to the muted blend of bird chatter, insect buzz and the slight wind rustling through the tree branches. Inhaling deeply, he savored the spicy sweet scent of roses, sun-warmed grass and woodsy bark, and wondered why he didn't spend more time out-of-doors.

The answer came as he looked at the baby again, then at Megan as she stepped out of the house and started toward him, two tall glasses of iced tea in hand.

He had all the time in the world now for quiet moments like this, but no one with whom to share them. Better to keep busy with work, even make-work, or to zone out in front of the blaring television set than sit all alone under a tree on a lazy Sunday afternoon.

"You're looking rather pensive," Megan said, a tentative smile hovering on her lips as she paused at the edge of the quilt and offered him one of the glasses she held. "Is there a problem?"

"Not at all," Jake hastened to assure her, taking the glass from her.

His fingers brushed hers, only momentarily, but the contact sent an electric jolt through him, and he almost sloshed tea onto the quilt. Megan, too, seemed to jump at their all-too-brief physical contact, then quickly turned away.

"Any progress finding Matthew's mother?"

Moving to the far end of the rose bed, she knelt down by the small patch of weeds that remained there. She gulped a few swallows of her tea, set her glass aside, then sat back on her heels, shoulders braced, as if awaiting the worst.

"None," Jake replied, his heart twisting in his chest when she bowed her head for an instant in obvious relief, then visibly relaxed. "We seem to be the only ones who saw her Friday morning, and even we didn't catch a glimpse of her face."

"So now what?" Megan glanced at him questioningly before setting to work pulling the last of the weeds.

"I'm going to contact the bus company first thing in the morning and get a list of passengers who bought tickets for travel routed through Serenity over the past few weeks. Maybe we'll come across a familiar name if she actually arrived in Serenity by bus. She could have just been using a locker at the station to stow her things while she brought the baby here."

"I didn't realize that finding her would be quite so involved."

Sitting back again, Megan tied up the ends of the black plastic trash bag into which she had been tossing the weeds she'd pulled, then stood slowly.

"Actually, there's a fairly good chance that finding her is going to be impossible, especially if she doesn't want to be found."

Seeing that Megan intended to haul the unwieldy bag to the trash can standing near the garage, Jake scrambled to his feet and crossed the small patch of lawn separating them.

"Here, let me dump that for you," he said, taking the bag from her.

"Thanks."

She dusted her hands on the seat of her denim shorts, picked up her glass and walked over to the quilt. Pulling off the straw hat she'd been wearing, she looked down at the baby, a frown furrowing her forehead.

"I really want his mother to be found," she said, sounding as if she was trying to convince herself as much as him.

More aware than ever of the dilemma she faced, Jake stowed the plastic bag in the trash can, then joined her under the tree. Meaning only to comfort her for the briefest of moments, he touched her shoulder.

"I know you do, Megan."

Startled, she glanced up at him. He saw, at once, the sadness shadowing her eyes, and the longing. Unable to stop himself, he slipped an arm around her, drawing her close to his side. To his surprise, she uttered a shaky sigh and leaned against him with seeming gratitude, clutching her glass in both hands as if hanging on to it for dear life.

"And I really *don't*," she admitted, revealing the true depth of her conflict in a whisper-soft voice.

"I know that, too." He brushed his lips against her soft curls, slightly damp but still sweetly scented, even after being stuffed under the straw hat.

"I realize that he's not my baby to keep," she insisted. "He has a mother who surely would have been more careless about where she left him if she didn't love him, and he belongs with her. But in my heart, I can't help hoping that somehow, some way, I won't have to give him up in the end. Crazy, isn't it?"

"Not really. You want what you believe is best for Matthew—a reunion with a mother who loves him. But that might not be possible. In which case, what harm is there in your wanting the chance to love him and mother him yourself?" Jake asked, reaching out with one hand to tilt her face so he could look her in the eye.

She gazed at him questioningly, seeming not quite ready to be reassured of her basic decency, then glanced away.

"None, I suppose," she conceded.

"So stop being so hard on yourself." He hugged her closer and playfully pressed another kiss on the top of her curly head.

"I'm not. I'm just admitting to a certain amount of selfishness."

"There you go again, using a negative instead of a positive," he teased. "Why not say you're admitting to an amazing generosity of spirit toward an abandoned baby and his wayward mother?"

"Because I'm not that good a person," she retorted, her tone turning caustic.

"To me, you are. You always have been."

"What a convenient attitude for you to have had. One that made life easy for you—didn't it? Good old Megan, she not only can—she *will*—handle anything. No need to stick around—" She broke off abruptly and shrugged away from him.

Baffled by her sudden change of mood, Jake eyed her uncertainly. Then, as he realized how she had twisted his words, a surge of anger rolled through him.

"I had a job that took me away from home. I continued working at that job after our son was born because you didn't seem to have any problem with it. Believe me, it was never easy leaving you and Will. But sometimes it was hard coming home. You were so damned self-sufficient. After a while you didn't really seem to need me much at all."

"That's not true, Jake." She whirled around to face him, her eyes flashing. "I wanted you there. I *needed* you there." As quickly as she'd turned on him, she turned away again, adding quietly, "I just didn't feel I had the right to interfere with your work by saying so."

"What was I supposed to do? Read your mind?" He put his hands on her shoulders and forced her to face him.

"No, of course not," she admitted in a low tone, though she refused to meet his gaze.

"I've said that I'm sorry about leaving you alone with Will. I've said that I wished I'd made better choices after he was born. What more do you want from me, Megan? I can't turn back time...much as I'd like to."

"I don't want anything more from you, Jake, anything at all." She stepped back, once again shrugging off his hold on her. "Except your help finding Matthew's mother."

Jake didn't believe her. Not after the way she'd kissed him Friday night, and not after the way she'd accepted his comfort only a few minutes ago. She hadn't hardened her heart to him quite as much as she wanted him to think. But he knew he'd pushed her as far as he dared that afternoon.

"You've got it, and more," he said.

She glanced over her shoulder, her gaze cool and dismissive, but before she could say anything else, Matthew stirred on the quilt, drawing their attention as he awakened from his nap. Blinking his blue eyes several times, he stared up at them, then screwed up his little face and let out a yowl.

Megan knelt down beside the baby, setting her glass aside.

"Oh, sweetie, don't cry," she crooned, lifting him into her arms. "I'm here, and I have a bottle all ready for you."

Gracefully, she rose to her feet again, her composure even more firmly back in place. Facing him, she offered a polite smile that didn't quite make it to her eyes.

"Thanks for stopping by," she said.

"You're welcome," he replied, aware that he was being dismissed, yet again.

Much as he didn't like it, Jake couldn't see any way around it, though. He had done what he'd come to do. There was no reason for him to stay any longer. Not without an invitation, the likelihood of which was zero to none.

Once again, Megan had distanced herself from him, withdrawing what little trust she'd felt toward him as he'd held her close. All he could do without causing a scene was quietly walk away.

"You'll let me know about the list of passengers

from the bus company, won't you?'' she asked as he turned away.

''I'll want you to take a look at it, if you don't mind,'' he answered, heading toward the gate.

''Oh, no, I don't mind.''

''I'll be in touch, then.''

Quelling the urge for a last glance at her and the baby, Jake let himself out of the yard. The rest of the day loomed ahead of him—the same lovely day he'd appreciated so much an hour ago. Only now he was alone again.

Chapter Seven

On the Saturday evening following Jake's Sunday afternoon visit to her house, Megan, pushing Matthew's stroller, walked toward St. Mary's Catholic Church with Margaret Griffin. Though she was looking forward to the Church's annual picnic, her thoughts kept drifting back to the past week. As had happened several times since last Sunday, Megan replayed in her mind the moment of weakness she'd had with Jake. She had done so well, or so she thought, hiding the inner leap of joy she'd experienced when she had seen him standing on her front porch. And alone with him in her backyard, she'd finished the weeding, grateful for a task that allowed her to keep her distance while she ever-so-slowly regained her composure.

He had come to the house only to report on his

investigation. She knew it was foolish to make any more of his presence there than that. In fact, she hadn't *wanted* to make any more of it. She had stopped depending on Jake two years ago, and she wasn't about to start again, except where finding Matthew's mother was concerned. That wasn't personal, though. At least, it hadn't been until she leaned against him so trustingly when he put his arm around her shoulders.

Then one thing had led to another, just as it had Friday night. First she had welcomed the comfort he offered her, mellowing at the warmth of his touch, the understanding in his tone. She hadn't been able to hide from him her feelings about the baby—feelings that were both confusing and conflicting. And she had been heartened by the words of encouragement he'd spoken.

From one moment to the next, she'd gone all bristly, though, like a porcupine spreading its quills at the slightest hint of danger. For the second time in less than seventy-two hours, she had spoken of Jake's many absences after Will's birth, dredging up the pain and anger she had suffered in the past, and planting it firmly between them in the present as a means to ward him off.

That he had made sense, pointing out to her that he wasn't a mind reader, had only irritated her even more. How dare he make his negligent behavior *her* fault?

He really hadn't, though. He'd taken responsibility for the choices he'd made, and he had apologized sincerely for the hurt he had caused her. Unfortunately, by the time she had settled down enough to realize it, he was long gone.

"Oh, here's a good spot," Margaret Griffin said, interrupting Megan's reverie.

She gestured toward one of several folding tables surrounded by four chairs that had been grouped together on a shady patch of lawn under a cluster of trees on the church grounds.

"Perfect," Megan agreed.

"Why don't we claim a table? Then we can take turns going through the buffet line."

The picnic was well under way that Saturday evening, and a fair-size crowd had already gathered to sample the grilled chicken and smoked brisket, potato salad, corn on the cob and coleslaw, not to mention the veritable smorgasbord of desserts provided by the ladies of the parish.

"Good idea," Megan replied, wheeling Matthew's stroller ahead of her as she moved toward the table Margaret indicated. "Why don't you keep an eye on the baby while I fix plates for both of us? He should nap at least another thirty minutes or so."

"That would be lovely, dear." Margaret settled onto a chair with a sigh that sounded much relieved. "I'd forgotten how long a walk it is from my house to the church."

"Are you feeling okay?"

Megan eyed her friend with concern. Perhaps she should have insisted on taking her car, even though Margaret had said a walk in the evening air would do her good.

"I'll be fine after I've sat for a little while, but I'm

afraid by then there will be slim pickings left at the buffet table.''

"Chicken or brisket?'' Megan asked as she made sure Matthew's stroller was within easy reach of Margaret's chair.

"Brisket, please, with all the fixings.''

"I'll be right back.''

Her thoughts drifting to Jake again, Megan headed for the end of the line of people eagerly waiting their turn to be served. She had assumed he would be at the picnic in an official capacity, if nothing else. She had seen two of his officers already. One had been directing traffic, the other standing near the counter where the meal tickets were being sold. But Jake didn't seem to be anywhere around. Which was just as well.

She was getting too used to having contact with him of one kind or another. And though she took pains not to let him know it, every time she saw him, or talked to him on the telephone, she found herself looking forward to their *next* encounter even more.

Like she was now, she mused with a wry smile as she once again scanned the crowd.

No matter that she had run him off in anger both times she'd allowed him to hold her close. His kisses and caresses had opened the door to her soul—a door that should have remained closed. And much to her chagrin, that original opening seemed to have inched wider each time she'd had even the slightest contact with him in the days that followed.

Mostly, he had called to update her on the progress, or lack thereof, in his search for Matthew's mother.

A couple of times, however, he had stopped by the house, once late in the afternoon with the list of bus passengers for her to review, and once early in the evening. On both occasions the baby had been awake, and Jake had gone out of his way to pay attention to him. But he hadn't stayed long—at least, not as long as Megan would have liked. Though, in all fairness, she hadn't given him a reason to.

She hadn't asked him to stay for dinner or to sit with her on the porch swing and have a drink as the sun set. She'd exchanged a few cool and distant pleasantries with him, and when he had said that he'd better be on his way, she had let him go.

Just as she should have, Megan reminded herself as she took her place at the end of the line snaking toward the buffet tables. She might still have feelings for Jake—well, okay, no *might* about it. But she wasn't going to let herself be ruled by them. She'd only end up getting hurt again.

Ahead of her a little way, she saw Steven Barns, the high school principal, along with the older of his two daughters and her fiancé. Glancing back at her, Steven smiled and waved her forward, indicating that she should join him. At the same instant, she felt the touch of a hand on her shoulder.

After returning Steven's smile with a negative shake of her head—she hated it when others cut into a line, and she wouldn't do it herself—she turned to see Jake standing right behind her. Obviously attending the church picnic as Chief Cahill rather than just Jake, he looked unusually handsome in the uniform of black pants and khaki, short-sleeved shirt he rarely chose to wear.

"Wow, I hardly recognize you," she teased, speaking her thoughts aloud before she could stop herself. "You certainly do clean up nice."

"I could say the same about you," he replied, his tone just as devilish as he trailed a finger down the bare skin of her back revealed by the pale blue, thin-strapped sundress she wore.

Flustered by his compliment, the obvious admiration in his eyes, and the warm touch of his hand, Megan blushed and looked away.

"Thanks," she murmured, then took a steadying breath. "I thought you might be working this evening."

"Mostly supervising, although the other officers on duty don't really need looking after."

"Good for public relations to be seen, I suppose," Megan ventured as the line moved forward and she collected a paper plate for herself and one for Margaret from the waiting stack.

"Very good." Jake tapped one of her plates with a finger. "Are you here with someone?"

"Margaret Griffin." Megan gestured to where her friend sat, noting that she'd been joined by Jilly Maitland, who was holding Matthew. "What about you?"

"No, I'm on my own for the evening," he answered, just wistfully enough to give Megan pause.

He had grown up in Serenity and he still had friends in town, many of them already at the picnic. He was also the chief of police, a position that would have afforded him a welcome among the members of the business community and the city council, also in attendance. Yet he sounded as lonely as she often felt even among her students and the few friends she'd made. As if a part of him were missing—a part that couldn't be replaced by just anyone.

As she held out the plates for the various servers to fill, Megan mentally argued the pros and cons of inviting Jake to join them at their table. People would talk if he sat with them, but no doubt people would talk just as much or more if he didn't.

Everyone knew he was searching for the mother of the baby abandoned on her front porch. It would seem odd for them to avoid each other under the circumstances. And, in all honesty, she *wanted* his company, and it was better for her peace of mind to have it out in public than alone in the privacy of her home.

"Would you like to sit with us at our table?" she asked after a last moment's hesitation. "We have plenty of room."

"I'd like that a lot," he replied, his tone so fervent that she glanced at him in surprise.

"Me, too." Unable to stop herself, she spoke her thoughts aloud as she met his gaze, then quickly turned away, even more flustered than she'd been earlier.

What on earth was wrong with her? She was acting as if she was *thrilled* that he wanted to sit with her at the church picnic. Only, she wasn't acting at all, she admitted with a wry twist of her lips as she led the way to their table.

Jake set his plate down, said hello to Margaret and

Jilly, who was still holding Matthew, then went off to get soft drinks for all of them.

"I can take the baby while you go through the buffet line," Megan said, glancing at Jilly. "I'm getting pretty good at juggling him and eating at the same time."

"Oh, no. You enjoy your meal. I'll take him for a little walk around the grounds." Jilly waved to a group of her friends who had just arrived, then eyed Megan questioningly. "If that's all right with you?"

"That's fine, Jilly. Thanks a lot."

"She certainly seems to like that baby," Margaret commented as Jake joined them again, drinks in hand.

"Who's that?" he asked. "Jilly?"

"She's been at Megan's house almost every day the past week," Margaret told him, taking a forkful of her brisket.

"She's just feeling lonely and at loose ends," Megan added by way of explanation, digging into her chicken, as well. "Her parents were only home for the weekend, then they took off for the American Medical Association conference in San Francisco, followed by a few days of vacation in Hawaii."

"Odd that they didn't include her," Jake commented, obviously surprised.

"She was supposed to spend the summer in Chicago instead of coming home. She had a lot of trouble with her organic chemistry class and ended up dropping it. She was going to take it during the summer session, then changed her mind at the last minute. By then, it was too late for them to get a plane ticket for her. She doesn't seem to mind missing out on the trip, though. I gather there's a storm brewing about the decision she's made to change majors, and she'd just as soon put it off as long as possible. Seems she's decided she doesn't want to go to medical school, after all, and she knows her parents aren't going to be happy about it.''

"Maybe not at first, but surely they'll come around,'' Margaret said. "She's such a delightful young woman, and the times I've seen her with her parents, it's obvious they love her dearly.''

"I'm sure you're right,'' Megan agreed. "They'll be home in another week or so. In the meantime, I've been glad to have her company.''

"Mine, too, I hope.'' Margaret smiled as she scooped up the last of her potato salad.

"Yours, and Alice Radford's, and most of my nearest neighbors'. And Jake's, too.'' Megan shot a tentative smile his way, and he returned it as he pushed his empty plate aside.

He had been silent during most of the meal, seeming content to listen as she and Margaret discussed Jilly's plight.

"I've tried not to wear out my welcome by coming around *too* often,'' he said, shooting a wry glance Megan's way.

"Oh, I don't think that's possible, is it, Megan?'' Margaret asked, her eyes twinkling, obviously ignoring the fact that they had been divorced for the past two years, and it would actually be more likely that she'd prefer *not* to have Jake hanging around.

"Jake is welcome to stop by any time,'' she stated primly as she stood and gathered their empty plates.

"As long as I'm there on official business," he quipped, standing, too, and taking the paper plates from her to toss in a nearby trash can.

Again, Megan detected a wistful note in his voice that she couldn't dismiss.

"Well, that *is* the only time you've come to the house—to report on your investigation," she reminded him, a defensive edge in her own tone.

"*Lately.*" He emphasized the single word, then quietly held her gaze before checking his watch. "Looks like it's about time for me to make the rounds. Ladies—" he nodded, first to Margaret, then to Megan "—I've enjoyed your company."

As Jake ambled off into the crowd, Serenity's own polka band began to play under an awning set up near a makeshift plywood dance floor. Watching him walk away, Megan experienced a pang of regret for the present as well as the past. She kept letting Jake walk away when she wanted him to stay simply because she couldn't seem to say what was in her heart. The possibility that he would leave her, anyway, had been, and still remained, too great.

"Hi, again," Jilly sang out, dancing up with Matthew, who was obviously enjoying the bounce and sway of her steps.

"You'd better get something to eat before the food's all gone," Megan said, grateful for the distraction. Taking the baby from her, she swayed to the music as Jilly had been doing.

"You're right," Jilly agreed. "I'll be back in a few minutes."

While Jilly ate, various people stopped at their table to visit, among them Steven Barns. After a few minutes of polite conversation, he asked Megan to dance. Seeing no way she could refuse without seeming rude, she let Margaret take the baby, then followed him reluctantly onto the dance floor.

To her surprise, she had a wonderful time, whirling around with him to the lively music. He was such a nice man, kind and decent and devoted to the students and faculty at the high school. Megan wished she could be interested in him in the same way he seemed to be interested in her. But she knew she never would be. She still cared too much for Jake.

She danced several dances with Steven. Then, to her amazement, Jake cut in at the start of a slower, more sedate waltz, stealing her from the high school principal with a courtliness to which the other man couldn't take offense.

Megan thought otherwise, however.

"That wasn't very nice," she reprimanded, refusing to meet Jake's gaze as he led her around the dance floor at much less than the arm's length she would have greatly preferred.

"No, it wasn't," he admitted with a decidedly masculine chuckle. "But I'm glad I did it, anyway."

Squeezing her hand, he drew her even closer.

Megan tensed a moment, then gave in, savoring the ripple of his muscles under the hand she'd placed on his shoulder. Dancing with Jake had always been a pleasure, and it still was. They suited each other in height and build, and his sense of rhythm melded with hers completely.

"I thought you had to work," she said after a few

seconds, unable to bear the sexual tension created by their mutual silence.

Better to make small talk than to think about the way his breath tickled her ear and warmed her cheek, his chest grazed against her breasts, and his hand tightened at her waist as he drew her closer still.

"I'm currently searching the dance floor for signs of criminal activity," he replied, his voice soft and teasing.

"Found any?"

"Over to the right... Mr. Lundsford just trampled Mrs. Lundsford's foot for the third time."

"I say lock him up."

"And your neighbors, the Bukowskis, refuse to give up and go back to their seats even though they are living proof that some people have no rhythm."

"Jake, you're terrible."

Laughing in spite of herself, Megan looked up at him. He gazed back at her, his eyes sparkling with mischief. Then, lifting her off her feet and twirling her around, he hugged her hard.

More aware than she'd been of his masculine appeal, and suddenly feeling threatened by it, she sobered immediately. As he set her on her feet again, she stepped away from him purposefully, throwing them both out of step as the music came to an end.

"Hey, sorry about that," he said, looking slightly bemused. "Guess I got a bit carried away. But it was so nice dancing with you again...."

"It was nice dancing with you, too. For old times' sake," she replied in a dismissive tone.

Focusing on one of his shirt buttons rather than

look him in the eye, Megan clasped her hands together and took another step back. She didn't want Jake getting carried away around her. The temptation to go along with him would be too great, and she knew all too well where that could lead.

As she stood amid the milling crowd on the dance floor, Megan's heart fluttered as she recalled the passionate kiss they'd shared Friday night.

"Yes, of course, for old times' sake," Jake agreed with just the slightest hint of sarcasm.

She flashed a questioning look at him and he eyed her steadily for a long moment, then took her by the arm and turned her toward the sidelines where Steven waited patiently.

"Don't patronize me, Megan. I deserve better than that from you, and you know it."

"I wasn't—" she began.

"You were," he cut in, his voice pitched low, his words for her ears only. "You liked dancing with me, right here, right now. You liked it a lot."

Unable to deny the truth he spoke, she crossed the dance floor with him, her face burning.

"Thanks for the dance," he said as they reached the sidelines, then nodded to Steven, turned and walked away.

"Are you up to another polka?" Steven asked.

"Sure," Megan agreed, willing to do anything that might take her mind off Jake and how easily he could push her buttons.

She had wanted to believe she was well and truly over him. Now she knew for a fact that she probably never would be.

Megan danced twice more with Steven, though her heart wasn't in it, then begged off to rejoin Margaret and Jilly at their table. As the three of them sat together, enjoying the music a little while longer, she watched Jake moving easily from group to group, stopping to talk a few minutes here, then a few minutes there. He was popular around town, and rightly so. And a good man, too, she admitted. The snooty comment she'd made to him after they'd danced had been way out of line.

When Matthew began to fuss, Jilly offered to drive everyone home in her little car. Margaret accepted gratefully, but Megan decided she would rather walk. Twilight had only just begun to fall, the evening was especially fine, and she knew the baby would settle down once she put the stroller into motion.

As Jilly drove off with Margaret, and she set off down the sidewalk, Megan heard Jake call her name.

"Are you heading home?" he asked, falling into step beside her.

"Yes, it's time," Megan replied, barely hiding her surprise that he'd come after her. "Matthew has already lasted longer than I expected."

"I could give you a lift."

"Jilly offered, too, but it's such a nice evening that I feel more like walking."

"Mind if I walk along…unofficially?"

Megan smiled at Jake's teasing tone. They hadn't parted on the best of terms out on the dance floor, but to her relief he didn't seem to be holding it against her. Her heart also warmed at his pointed use of *unofficially*.

He wanted her to know that he wasn't just doing his duty by seeing her home, and that pleased her more than she liked to admit. Maybe if she tried not to let their past history intrude, they could be present-day friends.

"I don't know if that's possible since you're in uniform, Chief Cahill," she teased back, determined not to allow the moment to turn serious.

"Trust me, it is."

"All right, then."

"I could push the stroller, too."

"Unofficially?"

"By all means."

With a rueful shake of her head, Megan allowed Jake to take over for her. Walking along beside him down the quiet, tree-lined street, a gentle breeze teasing through her curls and lifting the hem of her dress, she looked down at Matthew, wide-eyed but momentarily tranquil, and savored the sudden sense of contentment that settled over her.

It was just a moment in time, she reminded herself again. One moment with Jake and Matthew that wouldn't last forever. But that was no reason not to make the most of it. Especially when she finally felt as if all was right with her world.

Chapter Eight

Jake knew better than to make more of Megan's mellow mood than he had a right to. Just because she had invited him to sit with her at the picnic, had agreed to dance one dance with him, and was now allowing him to walk her home, he didn't dare let himself believe her heart had softened toward him in any measurable way.

Well, he *shouldn't* allow himself to believe it, he amended as he guided the stroller down Megan's street, carefully keeping his pace slow to lengthen their time together. He could say something without thinking, set her off again just like he had on the dance floor, and be banished from her presence in an instant.

But hope was a hard thing to let go of where Megan was concerned. Even after so much time had gone by—time they had spent painfully far apart.

The role he had to play in finding Matthew's mother, a very necessary role, had allowed him to bridge that gap, if only temporarily. Once he had done his job, though, Megan could, and probably would, distance herself from him once more. Which made it all the more difficult for him to acknowledge that he hadn't offered to walk Megan home for the pleasure of her company alone.

He had tossed out the word *unofficially* more to lighten the moment than to mislead her. In fact, there were a few questions he wanted to ask her—questions he hoped wouldn't cause her any undue concern. They were more the result of a hunch he'd had than anything else, but still he felt obligated to ask them. As for his growing suspicions...those he planned to keep to himself, at least until he had something more substantial to justify them.

To Jake's relief, Megan seemed to take for granted that he would come inside the house. Without the slightest hesitation, she sent him to the kitchen to warm Matthew's bottle while she took the baby upstairs to change his diaper.

Just as they routinely split such mundane tasks between them, he thought, a smile tugging at the corners of his mouth as he opened the refrigerator door.

"Would you mind giving him his bottle, too?" Megan asked as she joined him in the kitchen a few minutes later. She had dressed Matthew in a white knit sleeper dotted with tiny blue sheep similar to the ones Will had worn. "Unless you have to go back to St. Mary's…"

"I just happen to be off duty for the night. And I'd like very much to give Matthew his bottle."

Jake took the baby from her, handling him much more comfortably than he had that first Friday night. Sitting in one of the chairs by the kitchen table, he reached for the bottle of formula he'd warmed. Eagerly, Matthew latched onto the nipple and began to nurse.

"This little guy sure has a hearty appetite," he commented, chuckling softly as he gazed at the baby.

"I learned right away that he doesn't like missing a meal even by a few minutes," Megan said as she emptied the diaper bag, then rinsed out the bottles she'd taken to the picnic. "Luckily, I've had an extra pair of hands around here to help out most days since I'm still not quite up to par on the multitasking of baby care."

Picking up on the opening she had unconsciously given him, Jake asked casually, "You mean Jilly Maitland?"

"Margaret Griffin, too, and Mrs. Bukowski from across the street, and, of course, Alice Radford. But, yes, mostly Jilly. I know it's selfish of me, but I'm so glad her parents have been gone the past week. Not only has she been a big help to me, she actually seems to enjoy spending time with Matthew, too. He loves all the attention she gives him, and he always naps so much better after she's been here."

The easy way in which she gave out information about Jilly indicated to Jake that Megan hadn't yet suspected, even for an instant, that the young woman might have another reason—aside from too much time on her hands—to visit the baby so regularly. Just as well, too, he thought as Matthew, eyes closing, finished the last of his formula.

Jilly Maitland might *not* have another reason.

"You said she was one of your best students...."

"She, Amanda Lawler and Christina Evans. What a threesome they were, and still seem to be. They made my first year teaching at Serenity High School worth all the work of starting over somewhere new."

Though Megan made the last comment in a matter-of-fact tone, Jake saw the flash of sadness in her eyes as she obviously recalled why she had returned to Serenity. But she seemed to set aside the memory briskly enough as she closed up a disposable-diaper-filled trash bag and set it outside the backdoor.

"Did they keep in touch with you after they went away to college?" he pressed on, trying not to sound more than moderately interested.

"I heard from each of them several times during the first semester, but then, hardly at all after the Christmas holiday. I was really surprised to see them Saturday afternoon. Pleased, too, of course." She paused beside Jake and touched his shoulder. Then, as if realizing what she'd done, she quickly drew her hand away. "I'd better take him up to bed," she said, not quite meeting his gaze as a hint of a blush stained her cheeks.

"I'll do it," Jake replied.

Heartened by the fact that the familiarity they'd once shared still seemed to come easily to her even though she'd rather it didn't, he stood and started toward the kitchen doorway. He wanted to ask Megan if she'd ever been especially friendly with the girls' parents—the Maitlands in particular—but he didn't want to arouse her curiosity by pressing her any further about them. Knowing her, she would then be the one asking questions he wasn't ready to answer yet.

Megan trailed after him up the stairs to the baby's room, then crossed to the dresser to turn on the nightlight as he gently tucked Matthew into the crib.

"Will he sleep until morning?" Jake asked, drawing a light blanket over the baby's legs.

"I'm not sure." Megan moved to stand beside him. "I've been giving him a bottle at six or six-thirty in the evening, then another at eleven, then he sleeps until six or so in the morning. But we got off schedule tonight. It's almost eight-thirty, so either he'll be up at three or he'll sleep until five or five-thirty. I can live with five in the morning, but three o'clock…" She made a face as she turned to leave the room. "No, thanks."

After a last, lingering look at the sleeping baby, Jake followed Megan out to the hallway, then walked with her down the stairs. Though her mood still seemed companionable enough, he fully expected her to steer him toward the front door, as subtle an indication that it was time for him to be on his way as she was likely to deem necessary.

Instead, to his most pleasant surprise, she paused in the entryway and glanced up at him.

"I could make some coffee," she offered too warmly to be merely polite. "And I have an apple crumb pie that Mrs. Bukowski brought over the other day. I noticed that you didn't have time for dessert at the picnic. Unless there's somewhere else you need to be, or something else you need to do…'' Her words trailing off, she looked away nervously.

Jake wanted to reach out, to touch her cheek, to take her in his arms and sooth the distress he'd so obviously stirred in her. But he tucked his hands in his pockets and kept his distance. She could just as easily shrug off his attempt to comfort her as accept it, and another rebuff now would only set him back in his crusade to win her favor. He didn't want her chasing him away just yet. Hell, he didn't want her *ever* chasing him away again.

"Pie and coffee would really hit the spot right about now," he said, offering her an appreciative smile. "Need some help in the kitchen?"

"I can manage." She gestured toward the front door. "Why don't you go out on the porch? It's such a nice evening, we might as well enjoy it."

Jake chose one of the two wooden rocking chairs rather than the porch swing. He would have preferred the intimacy of the swing, but he knew better than to think Megan would. At least they could sit side by side in the rockers with only the small, round wooden table between them.

Rocking slowly back and forth, waiting for her to join him, Jake tried not to dwell on any possible ulterior motives she might have had for her unexpected invitation. Those that crossed his mind weren't especially heartening.

Maybe she wanted to reestablish certain personal

boundaries that she'd let slide over the past week. Or maybe she wanted to chastise him again for cutting in on Steven Barns at the picnic. Though she hadn't seemed to mind when she was dancing with him, he recalled with a complacent smile. At least not until he'd gotten a bit carried away—

"You're looking rather pleased with yourself," Megan said as she came up beside him, balancing a tray with mugs, plates of pie, napkins and silverware on it.

"Just thinking you were right. It is nice out here tonight," Jake replied, standing to take the tray from her.

"I'll be right back with the coffee," she said as he set it on the table.

Sitting across from him a few moments later, she filled their mugs, then offered him a plate and fork. They ate in silence for a while, each rocking slowly in their chairs as twilight deepened into darkness around them.

"Good pie," Jake said at last, carefully scooping up the remaining bits of the crumb topping from his plate.

"Would you like another slice?" Megan asked.

"Better not."

He set his plate aside and reached for his mug. Megan did likewise, still seeming content not to talk.

Jake thought of all the things he could say to her here in the night. Things he should have said to her years ago. But tonight, of all nights, he didn't want to open those old wounds she'd obviously worked so hard to heal.

Talking about Will, about the pain of his loss and the guilt he had lived with everyday since his son's death, would go a long way toward easing *his* burden. But what would it do to Megan? She had her own memories to bear. And now she also had the responsibility of caring for Matthew weighing on her shoulders.

"How is your father doing?" she asked, her quiet voice drawing him back to the moment at hand.

He glanced at her and saw her looking at him with honest interest. He reached for the coffeepot and refilled their mugs.

"He's doing fine. Spending most of his time in Austin, though. He asks about you...." Jake admitted, then hesitated. He wasn't sure Megan would appreciate knowing that she was one of the main topics of their weekly conversations. "He always liked you a lot. Still does, actually."

"I always liked him a lot, too, and I still do," she said. "He always stops by to see me when he's in Serenity. He was so glad that you came back home, but I don't think he believed you would stay as long as you have."

"He said the same to me," Jake acknowledged with a wry smile. "Now he's got it in his head that I should run for mayor in the next election. He says it would be a good way to start working toward taking over his senate seat when he's ready to retire."

"Would you want to run for the state senate one day?" Megan asked, eyeing him curiously.

"Not me. I'm more than satisfied working in law enforcement."

"Even though there's not much excitement in Serenity?" Looking away again, she frowned thoughtfully. "After working undercover as an FBI agent, aren't you bored here, Jake?"

From her tone, Megan seemed no more than vaguely curious, but Jake sensed an underlying seriousness to her questions. He also knew that she wasn't ready yet to hear, much less believe the earnest answer he had to give her.

"I admit that some days I wouldn't mind a good, old-fashioned bank robbery followed by a car chase on the highway to liven things up," he quipped instead. "But most of the time I'm glad I don't have to deal with violent crimes on a daily basis anymore. It's enough to have to worry about drug and alcohol abuse among our teenagers, domestic disputes, not-so-petty theft, vandalism and the occasional major accident on one of the back roads." He paused a moment, then turned the tables on her, interested in how she liked the change of pace in Serenity. "What about you?" he asked. "Don't you miss teaching in a big, state-of-the-art high school with lots of money to spend?"

"With classes of thirty students or more? No thanks—I'm happy here. Although the drug and alcohol abuse you mentioned seems to be on the increase. Even in Serenity we have too many parents who are too busy to keep tabs on what their kids are doing at two o'clock in the morning."

"I've been thinking that I'd like to put together a program geared to public awareness—a series of interactive talks including parents, students, teachers and members of the police force,'' Jake said. ''Would you be interested in helping me?''

''Yes, of course, and I'm sure Steven Barns would help out, too.''

Jake would have rather worked only with Megan, but he had no reason to purposely exclude the high school principal.

''I'll give him a call first thing Monday morning and see what we can work out.''

''Let me know when you want to meet so I can arrange for a sitter.'' Setting her mug on the tray, Megan stood and brushed a hand down the skirt of her sundress.

Aware that their time together was over for the evening, Jake stood, as well. ''You'll be next on my list Monday morning,'' he promised, reaching for the tray.

Obviously ready for him to leave, Megan picked it up before he could.

''Thanks for walking me home,'' she said, moving away from him.

''My pleasure, ma'am,'' he replied as he opened the door for her.

''You'll call if you find out anything about Matthew's mother?''

''Of course.''

''Too bad we didn't come across a name we recognized on the list of bus passengers,'' she added without much conviction.

''It was a long shot.''

''Well...good night, then.''

''Good night, Megan.''

As she started to slip past him through the doorway, Jake caught her arm in a gentle hold, bent and kissed her on the cheek. Startled, she almost dropped the tray. Would have if he hadn't reached out a steadying hand.

"Oops," she murmured, looking up at him, her eyes wide, her lips too inviting to ignore.

"Yeah, oops," he muttered, as well. Then, unable to stop himself despite the possible repercussions, he kissed her on the mouth.

She didn't even try to resist. She angled her head obligingly and kissed him right back. He wished he could pull her close and feel her body molded snug against his, but he had both hands on the tray. With the blasted thing balanced between them, he didn't dare let go of it.

After several soul-stirring moments, he finally, reluctantly, raised his head, unconsciously bracing himself for an angry recrimination of one kind or another. Instead, Megan ducked her head shyly and turned away.

"Well, good night…again," she said, her voice barely above a whisper.

"Sleep well," Jake replied, letting go of the tray at last and taking a step back.

"Yes, you, too."

Maybe, he thought. Maybe tonight, holding close to his heart the memory of her breath catching in her throat and her eyes flashing, not in anger but in gratified surprise, he would finally sleep well for the first time in two years.

Chapter Nine

Megan tossed restlessly in her bed for the third night in a row. Since Jake had left her Saturday evening with yet another passionate kiss, sleep had been much more elusive than she would have liked.

She had been drifting off wearily enough after putting Matthew to bed, usually sometime between ten-thirty and eleven. Caring for an infant took a lot of energy, mental as well as physical, and she had other responsibilities to fulfill, as well. But staying asleep for more than a few hours at a stretch had been impossible. She'd simply had too much on her mind.

There was the work she had to do on the new curriculum for her Texas history class, a project she had been looking forward to, but would now just as soon not have been bothered with. She could only focus on it in fits and starts, during Matthew's shorter and shorter daytime naps. Evenings she was usually too worn-out to concentrate as fully as she knew she should to make a decent job of it.

The new drug and alcohol abuse task force that Jake, good as his word, had suggested to Steven Barns, and to which she would be contributing, was also making demands on her time and attention. Since the idea had been as much hers as it had been Jake's, and since she believed such an initiative was sorely needed in Serenity, she had agreed to compile a list of parents she thought would be most apt to support the task force and help with its start-up. Their first meeting had already been scheduled for Thursday evening. Jake had offered to pick her up at six-thirty and take her to Steven's house, and Jilly had agreed to baby-sit for Matthew.

Although Megan had talked to Jake on the telephone for a few minutes each day, she hadn't seen him again since Saturday night. He had been cordial enough when they spoke, asking about the baby, making small talk about nothing in particular, then finally, to her secret relief, reporting that he'd made no further progress finding Matthew's mother.

She knew she had no reason to expect any more of him. But after the time they'd spent together Saturday, first at the church picnic, then later on her front porch, and the seeming reluctance with which he'd left her after kissing her so tenderly, yet so forcefully…

With a sigh of frustration, Megan rolled onto her side and stared at the clock on the nightstand. It was almost two o'clock. She had to stop thinking about

Jake and the way he kept kissing her. Had to stop wondering what he was playing at when she knew well enough that he wasn't playing at all.

Jake had never been the type to toy with another person's emotions. He was too straightforward for that. Kissing her had been his way of comforting her—nothing more, nothing less.

He not only understood how complex her feelings for Matthew had become; he realized, as well, that she could use all the moral support she could get. Offering her a hug and a kiss had fixed so many problems for them in the past. Until they had drifted so far apart that hugs and kisses had become too few and much too far between.

Matthew had drawn them together again. But only temporarily, Megan reminded herself. Once his mother had been found and Matthew was reunited with her, Jake would no longer have any reason to call on the telephone or stop by the house.

Unless she gave him one.

"Stop thinking about him. Stop, stop, *stop*," she ordered herself, turning onto her stomach and burying her face in her pillow.

She had to get some sleep or she'd be useless in the morning. In fact, considering how tiring the previous day had been, she should be deep into dreamland by now.

Matthew had become fussier and fussier as the afternoon progressed. Even Jilly, who always seemed to know how best to keep him entertained, had had a hard time getting him to stop crying. Megan had reassured her that babies had bad days just like adults, but Jilly had still seemed really worried about him, all the same.

Since Matthew had eagerly taken his bottles and hadn't been running a fever or vomiting, Megan had been reasonably sure he wasn't sick. Though he was still a bit young to be cutting a first tooth, that could have been the problem. Just in case it was, she had asked Jilly to rub a finger along his front bottom gum, and that seemed to sooth him for a while.

Megan had been especially sorry to see Jilly go that afternoon. To give her credit, Jilly had offered to cancel her plans to drive to San Antonio with her friends to see a movie. But Megan had insisted she would be fine on her own with the baby. And she had been as long as she walked with him in her arms or rocked with him in one of the rocking chairs on the front porch, patting his back and cooing to him.

She hadn't been able to put him in his crib until almost midnight, when he'd finally given in to his exhaustion. Megan had gratefully crawled into bed herself after a quick shower, and she had slept deeply for all of two short hours.

Changing positions yet again, she flopped onto her back and stared at the ceiling. She had no idea what had awakened her. One moment, it seemed she had been in the midst of a dream she couldn't now recall. And the next, she had been blinking into the darkness of her bedroom, the memory of Jake's kiss wrapping around her, stirring a longing in her she couldn't discount no matter how determinedly she tried.

"No, don't go *there* again or you'll never get back to sleep," she warned herself in a fierce whisper.

Forcing her thoughts away from Jake, Megan focused on Jilly, instead. The young woman seemed to have become quite attached to Matthew over the past ten days, arriving earlier and staying later as the week progressed. Looking back, Megan realized Jilly had failed to stop by to visit only a day or two since the Saturday afternoon when she had come by with her friends, Amanda and Christine.

Of course, with her parents out of town, she must be feeling lonely. And Megan knew that most girls Jilly's age often fantasized about, not to mention romanticized, having a baby of their own.

The reality of twenty-four-hour-a-day, seven-day-a-week child care wasn't something they factored into the equation. They enjoyed the hugs and cuddles, the playtime and the dressing up in cute little clothes. But when the crying wouldn't stop and the diapers needed changing and their designer jeans ended up splotched with sour milk spit-up, they were ready to make a fast getaway.

Not Jilly, though. She hadn't hurried away at the first sign of unpleasantness, especially that afternoon when Matthew had been so cranky. In fact, as Megan had already acknowledged, *she* had been the one to urge Jilly to drive to San Antonio with her friends as planned.

Though Jilly had gone, she'd gone reluctantly. And the look of concern in her eyes as she'd handed over Matthew had seemed out of proportion to the situation.

For one fleeting moment, the strangest thought crossed Megan's mind.

Was Jilly Maitland Matthew's mother?

But no, that couldn't be possible…could it? She had a good home and loving, caring parents. While they might not have approved of their daughter having a child out of wedlock at the age of twenty, surely they would have helped her in any way they could—

A weak cry coming from the baby's room sent all thoughts of Jilly from Megan's mind. It was more than a whimper, but not quite the demanding squall Matthew usually let out when he was in need of a bottle or a fresh diaper.

Sitting up in bed, Megan tossed aside the blanket and swung her feet to the floor with an odd sense of urgency. To her increasingly more practiced ear, Matthew sounded like he wasn't feeling very well, at all.

Hurrying into his room, she went straight to the crib, guided by the night-light on the little dresser in the corner.

"What's the matter, sweetie?" she asked, looking down at him.

Waving his tiny fists weakly, Matthew screwed up his face and continued to cry.

Megan bent over the crib and scooped him up, nuzzling his neck as she cradled him against her shoulder. Immediately, she realized he was running a fever. His skin was much too hot and dry, and there was a wheezing in his breathing that she heard as she held him close.

"Oh, no…oh, baby, no," she murmured as a wave of panic washed over her.

This was how it had started with Will. First, he'd run a fever then he'd had trouble breathing. Only a mild respiratory infection the pediatrician had said, writing a prescription for antibiotics that hadn't helped.

But it had been something much worse—something that had progressed too far by the time she'd finally taken him to the emergency room that fateful night three years ago.

Now something similar was happening with Matthew—he, too, was running a fever and he was having trouble breathing. This time, she wasn't going to wait until a pediatrician could fit them into his busy schedule, though. This time she wasn't going to be fobbed off with a prescription and a pat on the shoulder. She was going straight to the emergency room with Matthew, and she was going to demand blood tests as well as a thorough examination.

While Matthew continued to cry, Megan changed his diaper and dressed him in a fresh sleeper. Then she laid him on her bed while she quickly pulled on a pair of jeans and a T-shirt. Images from the past raced one around another in her mind, almost paralyzing her with fear.

She couldn't lose another child as she'd lost Will. Just the thought of it made her hands shake and her knees go weak.

Alice Radford should have never entrusted her with Matthew's care. More to the point, *she* should have never accepted the responsibility. She should have had more sense. She had proved herself to be incompetent as a mother once already, hadn't she? Assuming that she could provide adequate foster care, especially for an infant, had been foolishness on her part.

Somehow Megan managed to collect her purse and car keys, and get Matthew settled in his car seat. The poor baby lay there quietly, obviously too ill to even cry anymore. The drive to the hospital, actually no great distance away, seemed to take forever, even though the streets of town were deserted.

Arriving at last, Megan parked as close to the emergency room entrance as she could, then carried Matthew into the brightly lit waiting room, her heart pounding.

She was surprised and dismayed to see an unexpected bustle of activity there. What could possibly be going on at such an early hour on a Tuesday morning? Vaguely, she noticed a police officer along with another man talking to a harried-looking, middle-aged couple on the far side of the room. Catching bits and pieces of their conversation, she realized there must have been an automobile accident on the interstate highway just outside of Serenity.

The clerk at the reception desk finished her telephone conversation as Megan halted before her, then glanced up with a distracted look on her face.

"Yes? Can I help you?" she asked.

"My baby's sick. He has a fever and he's wheezing. He needs to be seen by a doctor right away," Megan answered, not even trying to keep the terror out of her voice.

She knew she sounded as if she was on the verge of hysterics. The clerk would think she was certifiable. But then, working in an emergency room, the woman must be used to desperate pleas from desperate people.

"I'll need some information from you first, Mrs.—"

"Cahill, Megan Cahill. Can't I fill out the forms while the doctor sees my baby?" she asked as the woman held out a clipboard. Against her shoulder, Matthew stirred restlessly and whimpered in a way that tore at her heart.

"I'm sorry, Mrs. Cahill. The doctor on duty is busy with another patient at the moment. Have a seat, fill out the necessary paperwork, and one of the nurses will be with you just as soon as possible."

"But he's burning up with fever...."

"What's going on?"

Startled as much by the sound of Jake's voice as the touch of his hand on her shoulder, Megan whirled around to find him standing right behind her. He must have been with the police officer, talking to the middle-aged couple who were now seated in the waiting area. She'd seen them when she first arrived.

"Jake..."

She breathed his name with a sense of relief. He was here at the hospital. He would help her this time. She wouldn't be alone if the worst happened, as she was so afraid it would.

"Are you all right?" he asked, his eyes shadowed with concern.

"It's Matthew. He woke up a little while ago running a fever and wheezing. He's sick, Jake, really sick the way Will was. We have to have a doctor examine him immediately. Please, tell them we can't wait—"

"I will, Megan, I will." He put an arm around her shoulders and drew her close to his side, then leveled his gaze on the clerk. "How long do you think it will be?"

"I've already alerted one of the nurses. She's getting one of the examination rooms ready for you right now. Then she'll be able to take a look at the baby. In the meantime, why don't you have a seat and fill out the paperwork?" she advised in a matter-of-fact tone.

When Megan opened her mouth to protest, Jake squeezed her shoulder, turning her toward a row of chairs.

"Come on, Megan. Help me with the forms."

"But..."

"We're here at the hospital, and a nurse will be able to take a look at him shortly," Jake soothed. "He'll be all right until then."

Megan wanted to argue with him, to rail against him and his calm complacency. He hadn't sat in an emergency room with a sick child the way she had, waiting and waiting and *waiting*. He couldn't possibly understand how terrified she had been then, or how terrified she was now that history might be repeating itself, and she'd once again be responsible for the death of a child.

But what good would it do to turn on him? He was here with her tonight, he *was* trying to help and she needed him just as much now as she had three years ago.

As Megan sat beside Jake in one of the molded plastic chairs, she was vaguely aware that the woman she'd seen earlier was crying quietly on the other side of the waiting room. When Jake reached for the clipboard, she let him take it, and answered him as best she could when he read the questions aloud.

It took only a few minutes to complete the forms, then Jake returned the clipboard to the clerk. Sitting beside her again, he offered to hold the baby. Matthew had fallen asleep, though, and she didn't want to disturb him.

While the baby was still running a fever, much to Megan's relief, his condition didn't seem any worse than when she'd first taken him out of his crib. Glancing at Jake, she saw him looking at her, a frown furrowing his forehead. He must think she was crazy, the way she'd been behaving.

"I gather there was an automobile accident," she said, nodding toward the couple across the room. "Not fatal, I hope."

"No, thank God. But the Lerners' son was injured. He has a broken leg and a mild concussion. Looks like he fell asleep at the wheel, ran off the road and hit a tree. Luckily he was wearing his seat belt. He'll be on crutches for rest of the summer, but otherwise, he's going to be okay."

At that moment, the doctor on duty appeared, then headed toward the Lerners. A nurse followed close behind him, gesturing to Megan and Jake.

"I have a room ready for you," she said as they stood. "Let's take a look at your little fellow, Mrs. Cahill, and see how he's doing."

"You don't have to stay," Megan said, glancing at Jake. "I'll be okay now."

"I'm here, and I'd feel a lot better staying with you until we find out what's wrong with Matthew," Jake replied, his tone brooking no argument.

Megan didn't demur. She had wanted Jake to stay with her. She just hadn't wanted to make him feel obligated.

Gratefully, she followed the nurse to the examination room as Jake walked along beside her. And with Jake's arm around her shoulders, she stood close to him, savoring the comfort he offered her as the nurse undressed a now cranky Matthew and set about checking his vital signs.

The doctor Megan had seen in the waiting room joined them a few minutes later, and blood was drawn at Megan's insistence. The initial prognosis was a possible touch of bronchitis exacerbated by an ear infection. Neither illness, as Megan well knew, was life threatening at such an early stage.

Matthew was immediately given an injection of antibiotics to speed his recovery. The doctor also wrote a prescription for her to fill in the morning, and gave her a sample of infant-strength acetaminophen to help ease the baby's earache. He promised to call the following day with the results of the blood work, as well.

With a sense of relief, Megan thanked the doctor.

"I'll drive you home," Jake said as he walked with her out to the parking lot, his arm around her tucking her close to his side.

"Thanks, but I can manage," she assured him, smiling up at him gratefully.

"You're worn-out."

"So are you."

"I'm used to it. It comes with the job." At her car, he took the keys from her hand. "Let me take you home and help you get Matthew settled."

Megan couldn't resist the pleading look in Jake's eyes. In truth, she didn't want to resist it. She wanted his help, needed his help. She also liked having it. Liked it much more than she knew she should.

But she would only be hurting herself by refusing to give in to him now. She *was* worn-out, physically and emotionally. She wanted Jake to take her home. In fact, she *needed* Jake to take her home. She'd had an awful scare, and though there was a good chance she had overreacted, she still wasn't completely convinced that Matthew would really be all right.

Leaning on Jake for a little while longer wouldn't change their relationship—at least not in the long run. It would simply help her get through the rest of the night, and that, in turn, would make her that much stronger when it came time for her to face another day on her own.

"Okay, Jake," she agreed. Pausing beside her car, she tilted her head against his shoulder and savored the comfort of his masculine warmth. Then, as she eased away from him again, she added quietly, "I really appreciate it."

"It's nothing, Megan. Nothing at all," he assured her, an odd catch in his voice.

Looking away, he turned the key in the door lock.

Chapter Ten

Nothing compared to what I could have done, should have done, for you three years ago, Jake thought as he stood aside and waited for Megan to secure Matthew in his car seat.

He'd had no idea what she had gone through with Will. By his own choice, he had left her alone with a sick child, so he hadn't been available to take them to the emergency room when his son's condition deteriorated. And while he could have easily imagined how awful that night must have been for Megan, never once had he allowed himself to think about the terrifying time she'd spent waiting, in vain, for word that Will would be all right. Nor had he dwelled on how she must have felt the moment when she'd been told, instead, that their son had died.

He had been weighed down with enough guilt, as

it was. What good would it have done to rub his nose in his failings? He hadn't been there for Megan and Will and, bottom line, he couldn't change that. He could only try to get past it.

Or so he had told himself three years ago.

Tonight, however, he had gotten all too good a look at some of what Megan had endured while their son fought a losing battle to live. Not all, since Matthew's ear infection hadn't been life threatening. But enough for him to understand, at last, just how much she had needed him, and just how badly he had let her down.

As he'd talked with the Lerners about their son's accident, Jake hadn't realized that the woman he'd glimpsed out of the corner of his eye, hurrying into the emergency room, clutching a baby in her arms, was Megan. Then he had heard her voice, high and tight, bordering on the edge of hysteria, and fear had clutched at his gut.

His first concern had been for her. What had happened to bring her to the emergency room at such an early hour of the morning?

He had excused himself as quickly as he could, leaving the Lerners in the capable hands of one of his more experienced officers. Then he'd followed Megan to the reception desk. Listening in on her conversation with the clerk, he'd learned that it was Matthew who was ill.

One look at his former wife's face, though, and the relief that he'd felt, knowing she was all right, drained away. Quickly, he realized she could have dealt better with a personal problem than one involving the child consigned to her care.

For Megan, the trip to the emergency room with a sick baby was history repeating itself—the devastating past come back to haunt her in the worst possible way. There wasn't anything he could do to wipe away those painful memories. But he could be there for her, as he hadn't been in the past. And he could make sure, as he hadn't done three years ago, that good news or bad, she wouldn't have to face it all alone.

"You've been awfully quiet," Megan said, reminding him in a tentative voice that he hadn't spoken since he'd helped her into the car fifteen minutes ago.

"Just thinking," he admitted as he pulled into her driveway, though he had no intention of going into any further detail.

Now was not the time to talk about the past. Dawn was only a few hours away, and she looked almost as exhausted as he felt. One day very soon, though, he was going to have a long talk with her. He was going to tell her how sorry he was for the way he'd let her down. And he was going to acknowledge, at last, that he finally understood why she'd never been able to forgive him.

"Good thoughts or bad?" she prodded gently, one hand on the door handle.

"Some of each," he replied in a rueful tone. "What about you? You've been quiet, too."

"I'm feeling kind of…numb," she said. "Numb with relief, actually. I'm so glad Matthew's okay."

"Me, too."

No longer lulled by the car's movement, Matthew began to whimper.

"Oh, baby, we're home now," Megan crooned.

"I'll get him out of the car seat while you unlock the front door," Jake said.

"Thanks a lot." Shooting him a weary smile, she dug her house key out of her purse as she climbed out of the car.

In the house, Jake handed Matthew over to Megan so she could take him upstairs to change his diaper and give him a dose of the acetaminophen. At her suggestion, he went to the kitchen to warm a bottle in case the baby was hungry. Joining her in the baby's room, bottle in hand, a few minutes later, he gladly offered to feed him.

"But you've been up all night," Megan protested, patting the fussy baby's back as she held him against her shoulder. "Go home and get some sleep. Otherwise, you're going to be good for nothing tomorrow."

"I could say the same about you," Jake countered, taking Matthew from her despite her seeming reluctance to give him up.

"But I don't have a job to go to."

"You forget, my love. I'm the chief of police. If I want to take a day off, I can and I will," he reminded her in a teasing tone. "Let me help out with Matthew."

"He's really fussy. I'm not sure he'll sleep."

"Then I'll take him downstairs so you can get some rest."

"You won't leave without telling me, will you?" she asked, finally beginning to give in.

"No, of course not," he promised.

"Don't let me sleep too late, either," she insisted, still hesitant.

"Megan…" Jake shot her a stern look as Matthew cranked up the volume of his crying another notch. "Go to bed."

"Okay," she agreed at last, smiling sheepishly.

Down in Megan's living room, Jake tried sitting on the sofa to give Matthew his bottle, but he had only limited success. The baby took about half the formula and kept most of it down. He didn't seem to have much interest in sleeping, though. Rather, it seemed to Jake that he was fighting to stay awake just so he could let it be known how much he disliked having an earache.

Staying on the sofa with the baby once he'd had his fill of formula was totally out of the question. Matthew squirmed and cried, refusing absolutely to settle down. Only when Jake walked with him did he quiet down a bit. But every time Jake glanced at him, cradled snuggly against his shoulder, Matthew looked right back, his blue eyes wide open.

How many times had he walked the floor late at night with Will? Not many, Jake admitted. Maybe a handful, altogether.

Megan had insisted on getting up with the baby because even when Jake was home, he still had to go in to the office every morning. Since she wasn't working outside the home, she had felt it was only fair that she handle night duty as well as day duty.

What a strain that must have been for her, Jake now realized. Giving birth was no easy task. Then to come home from the hospital and have to face the unending demands of a newborn, twenty-four hours a day, seven days a week, all on her own...

No wonder she hadn't had any energy left for him. Maybe if he had insisted on sharing the work when he could, she wouldn't have felt so overwhelmed, or so abandoned, when he'd had to go off on an assignment.

Will had been as much his son as Megan's, and as much his responsibility as hers, too. But she had given him an easy way out, and he'd gladly taken it. The few times he'd walked the floor with Will it certainly hadn't been any picnic. Still, it came with the territory, and two parents sharing the work and the worry would have made it easier all around.

Just one more thing he would have to tell Megan he'd finally come to realize, Jake acknowledged. Just as soon as he had the chance.

The sky was just beginning to lighten when Jake saw that Matthew had finally fallen asleep. At the risk of waking him, Jake sat on the sofa wearily, then held his breath, waiting to see what the baby would do. When he slept on, Jake heaved a soft sigh of relief.

Shifting on the sofa, he stretched out as best he could, holding the baby securely against his chest, and took a good look around Megan's living room now that it was light enough to see more than shapes and shadows. As he had the first time she'd allowed him inside her house, Jake saw again the sparse way in which the room was decorated.

She had left behind all the furniture they had bought together when she moved out of their town house, yet she hadn't gone to any great lengths accumulating things of her own. As if she hadn't wanted to make her house a real home, just a place where she happened to live, Jake thought, his heart filled with sadness for her.

Megan had always wanted a home and a family, and since she had lost one, she must have thought that she'd be better off without the other, as well. The less she put of herself into the house on Bay Leaf Lane, the less she would have to lose down the line.

Jake couldn't blame her for feeling that way. She had suffered more than her fair share of losses already. First her parents when she was only a girl, then Will, and in a way, him, too, when he'd run from his guilt and his anguish over their son's death.

And soon there could be another loss, as well, if his suspicions about Jilly Maitland proved to be true.

Jake hadn't had any luck tracking down a birth certificate for a Matthew Maitland on Monday. Since he hadn't any clue what the baby's father's surname might be, that avenue of investigation seemed to have reached a dead end.

He had then compiled a list of hospitals in the Chicago area. Later today he planned to start calling each one personally to ask if anyone by the name of Jilly Maitland, or anyone fitting her description, had given birth to a baby boy about three months ago.

He knew that finding the proof he needed to link Jilly to the baby was a long shot. If she *was* Matthew's mother, she could have gone almost anywhere to have her baby.

In fact, he could probably save himself a lot of time, and the town a huge telephone bill, by simply talking to the young woman. But as the beloved only child of one of Serenity's most respected couples, she deserved the benefit of the doubt, at least for the time being.

Jake didn't want to upset Jilly or her parents needlessly, any more than he wanted to upset Megan. Keeping his own counsel for a few more days wouldn't hurt anyone as far as he could see. The baby was safe here with Megan, and Jilly, home for the summer, wasn't going anywhere for the next few months. And he had learned early in his law enforcement career not to point a finger at anyone until he could prove, irrefutably, that they were guilty.

With another weary sigh, Jake tipped his head against the sofa cushions and closed his eyes, the baby still snug and safe against his chest. He should probably try to put Matthew in his crib. But if he woke up and began to cry, Megan would wake up, too.

She really needed more rest than she'd gotten. And Jake didn't want her insisting on taking over the baby's care just yet. Especially since she would also insist that he go home and get some sleep.

He could doze here just as easily; actually, more easily since Megan was nearby. And he could give her a hand with the baby when she finally did get up. He could even drive over to the pharmacy to fill the prescription the doctor had given her so she wouldn't have to take Matthew out.

Hell, there were all kinds of ways he could insinuate himself into her life on the pretext of helping her with the baby. Only it wouldn't just be a pretext.

He wanted to be here with her and Matthew as he hadn't been there with her and Will. He wanted a second chance with her, and he would make one in whatever way he could for as long as he was able. Then maybe by the time Matthew's mother had been found and reunited with her baby, he and Megan would have finally begun to find *their* way back to each other, too.

Chapter Eleven

Megan awoke with the vague feeling that there was something she needed to do. Though still groggy with sleep, she realized it was later than she'd been used to getting up. Almost seven-thirty according to the clock on the nightstand, which explained why there was bright sunlight peeping through the slats of the miniblinds on her bedroom windows.

But she didn't feel nearly as rested as she should have after such a long night's sleep—

With a start, Megan sat up in her bed and shoved her fingers through her errant curls, remembering all that had happened the night before. Finding Matthew crying in his crib, his skin feverish; the drive to the hospital emergency room; Jake's calming presence at the hospital; his help with the baby here at the house...

Thanks to him, she had gotten at least a few hours of sleep. And obviously, from the peace and quiet surrounding her, Matthew had settled down, as well.

But why hadn't Jake awakened her already?

He had promised not to leave without telling her, and she trusted that he hadn't. But surely once he had tucked Matthew into his crib, Jake would have wanted to head for home.

Slipping out of bed, Megan grabbed the jeans and T-shirt she had dropped on the floor a few hours earlier and pulled them on. Then she padded, barefoot, down the hallway and peered into the baby's room. Seeing that the crib was empty, she turned toward the staircase, a frown creasing her forehead.

She hurried down the stairs, paused to glance into the living room, then went still, her breath catching in her throat.

Stretched out on the sofa as much as his long legs would allow, Jake lay sound asleep with Matthew, who was also asleep, cradled securely against his chest. The sight of the two of them together—the strength of one guarding the innocence and vulnerability of the other—filled Megan with such tenderness and such intense longing that her heart ached.

With his tousled, shaggy hair and his beard-shadowed face, Jake looked young and wild and free, the lines of pain and sorrow that had been etched into his face over the years smoothed away by the tranquillity that often came with the deepest rest. And Matthew, snuggled into the crook of Jake's arm, was the picture of trusting contentment—as if he knew, instinctively, that no harm would come to him as long as Jake was there to keep him safe.

How well Megan remembered that feeling, and how very, very much she had missed it in the years they had been apart. Only in his arms had she ever known true peace and true happiness.

How had she allowed so much distance to come between them all those years ago? And why had she maintained that distance after Jake returned to Serenity to win back her favor?

It had all boiled down to trust, she admitted. Trust in her own worth and trust in Jake's ability to honor that worth. She hadn't believed she had a right to ask Jake to put her and Will ahead of his job because she hadn't believed he'd actually do it.

Not asking for what she needed had been easier on her spirit than having her request refused, or so she had thought at the time. Just as it had been easier on her spirit to turn him away when he first came to Serenity than to open herself up to more hurt when life in the small town began to bore him, as she was so sure it would.

Jake could talk all he wanted about how glad he was that he'd returned to Serenity. But he could never convince her that his tenure there would be permanent. She had overheard enough at the police station that day she'd been there with Matthew to know that he'd been thinking about going back to the bureau. And that would mean a return to his old way of life where everything—and everyone—else came second.

She couldn't live that way again, Megan knew. She *wouldn't.*

Trying desperately to harden her heart where her ex-husband was concerned, Megan crept back up the stairs as quietly as she could. With the image of Jake sleeping on the sofa—the baby snuggled safely in his arms—fresh in her mind, it wasn't easy. But she didn't dare allow herself to nurture hopes that would eventually be dashed.

She pulled clean clothes from her dresser drawers, then went into the bathroom to take a shower. As she soaped up under the steamy spray, she imagined herself washing away all the warm, fuzzy thoughts she kept thinking about Jake.

He was a good man, kind and decent and caring in his own way. But he wasn't the man for her. She had changed since Will's birth; changed even more since his death. Her wants and her needs were different now. She simply couldn't trust that the same was true of Jake, no matter what he said or did.

As she stepped out of the bathroom, dressed in black shorts and a pale pink, candy-striped blouse, Megan heard the rumble of Jake's voice coming from the baby's room. Following the sound down the hallway to the nursery, she paused in the doorway and saw that Jake had Matthew on the changing table. He was deftly wiping the baby's bare bottom as Matthew gazed up at him placidly.

As if sensing her presence despite her quiet approach, Jake glanced over his shoulder, shot her a wry grin, then grabbed a fresh disposable diaper from the stack she kept handy on the tabletop.

"Did you get some sleep?" he asked as he diapered the baby.

"More than you, I have a feeling."

"I look that bad, huh?"

"Actually, you've looked worse." Megan crossed the room and stopped beside Jake as he snapped the baby's sleeper over the fresh diaper.

"Oh, yeah? When?" he asked.

"After a couple of weeks working undercover as a member of a biker gang. After a month living on the streets trying to catch a serial killer with a penchant for homeless men. After—"

"Okay, okay." Again Jake flashed a grin her way. "I've looked worse."

Turning his attention back to Matthew, he deftly lifted the baby off the changing table.

"Hey, pal, look who's here. It's our Miss Megan, looking exceptionally lovely despite the scare you gave her."

"Here, let me take him," she offered, her face warming at his compliment.

"I popped a bottle in the bottle warmer before I brought him upstairs," Jake advised as he handed over the baby. "It should be ready."

"He looks so much better this morning. And he doesn't seem to be running a fever anymore." Pressing her lips to Matthew's forehead, Megan felt how cool his skin was compared to the night before. "I'm beginning to think I overreacted," she admitted.

"Not at all," Jake assured her as they walked down the stairs together. "That dose of antibiotics the doc gave him at the hospital kept him from getting any worse. Which reminds me...we have to have his prescription filled. I'll run over to the pharmacy and get it for you before I head home.''

''Why don't you give Matthew his bottle while I fix some breakfast?'' Megan suggested. ''Then I can drop you off at the hospital since your car's still there, and go on to the pharmacy myself.''

''Hey, I don't want to put you to all that trouble.'' Jake halted in the kitchen doorway and shoved his hands in the side pockets of his jeans. ''I can run by the pharmacy, then have one of the guys at the station pick me up here and take me over to the hospital.''

''It's no trouble at all,'' she insisted, smiling as she held Matthew and the bottle out to Jake. ''But it's up to you. I'm making an omelet for myself, regardless. With mushrooms, tomatoes, cheese and fresh chives.''

Just the way you like, Megan thought, holding his gaze and willing him to stay. He had done an enormous favor for her and she wanted to repay him if only in a small way. And, truth be told, she didn't want him to leave just yet, either.

''All right, then,'' he agreed. ''As long as you're sure...'' A look of gratitude warmed his eyes as he shot her a crooked smile.

Taking Matthew from her, he settled into his usual chair by the kitchen table in a way that was becoming much too familiar, not to mention much too enjoyable for Megan's long-range peace of mind.

But it had been *her* idea, she chided herself as she quickly took eggs and veggies and cheese from the refrigerator.

The coffeemaker gurgled and sputtered on the

counter, blending with the faint sound of birds chirping just outside the kitchen window, but she and Jake hardly spoke at all while she fixed their omelet. The silence they shared was comfortable, though, and companionable, a gentle reminder of how easily and completely their personalities had always meshed.

Neither of them had ever gotten off to a fast start in the morning, preferring instead to savor the early hours of each new day at a leisurely pace. Eventually they would discuss their plans for the time they would spend apart, but only after they'd had a cup or two of coffee and something to eat.

Falling back into that old routine came so naturally to Megan. It also felt so right. She couldn't imagine spending her mornings with another man. More to the point, she didn't want to imagine it.

For a fleeting, not to mention truly perverse, moment, Megan thought of Steven Barns, acknowledging the growing interest in her he had shown lately. Then she gave a very firm, very negative shake of her head as she cut the finished omelet in half and slid a piece onto each of the two plates she'd set on the counter.

She liked Steven. He was a very nice man. But she would never feel about him the way she felt, or rather, *used to feel,* about Jake.

''What?'' Jake asked, his mellow voice cutting into her thoughts and making her jump.

While she hadn't forgotten he was right there with her, Megan *had* failed to take into account just how observant he could be when he put his mind to it. Obviously, he had been watching her from his place by the table, and had noted the visible signs of her inner dialogue without her even realizing it.

Scolding herself for being much too complacent in his company, Megan set the plates on the table, spared him a slight smile and turned back to the counter to fill their mugs with coffee.

"Oh, nothing," she said. "Just…thinking…"

"So I gathered." Jake set aside the empty bottle and shifted the now sleeping baby to his shoulder. As she returned to the table with their coffee, he eyed her questioningly. "Not good thoughts, though."

"Not bad, either." She paused beside him, but kept her gaze fixed on Matthew. Refusing to be led by his probing tone, she added, "Maybe I should take him upstairs and put him in his crib."

"He's okay where he is. I can manage just fine one-handed. No sense disturbing him, especially when he might wake up in a cranky mood."

Megan couldn't argue with that line of reasoning, and didn't. Instead, as they ate, she voiced, again, her gratitude for his help the night before.

"I was asleep as soon as my head hit the pillow," she admitted with a rueful grin, digging into her omelet. "I'm not sure how I would have managed on my own, as exhausted as I was."

"You managed on your own with Will just fine, and you did it more often than you should have," Jake reminded her, steadily meeting her gaze.

Yes, she had, Megan acknowledged, looking away. But she didn't want to talk about those days. Nor did she want to talk about Will. The anguish she had experienced in the hours leading up to his death was all too fresh in her mind after the scare she'd had with Matthew, and that anguish left her feeling more vulnerable than she liked.

"Sleepless nights and babies seem to go together," she stated lightly, pushing away her plate, her appetite gone. "More coffee?"

As she moved away from the table and stood, Jake reached out with his free hand and caught her by the wrist, his grip firm but gentle.

"Megan, please..." he began. "We have to talk about the past. We have to talk about what happened to Will and what happened to us. Otherwise, we'll never be able to mend what's been broken between us."

Glancing at him, she saw the beseeching look in his tired, red-rimmed eyes. Her heart skipped a beat as she realized exactly where he wanted their conversation to go. Not only back three years to a time so painful for her that she had vowed never to revisit it with him, but also into the future.

She couldn't go there with him. She didn't have the trust necessary to bolster a lasting relationship. Nor did she have the heart to risk being disappointed by him all over again.

"We've been getting along well enough, all things considered," she pointed out, keeping her tone breezy as she eased her wrist free of his hold. "At least we're friends again."

"Are you satisfied with just being friends?" he demanded, then answered without giving her a chance. "I don't think so. Not the way you've kissed me."

"You caught me during some of my weaker moments,'' she shot back, a blush heating her face. ''Believe me, I was sorry afterward.''

''Oh, yeah?'' he challenged.

''Yeah.''

Setting her plate on the counter, she reached for the coffeepot with a shaking hand.

''Look, Jake, we've both had a long night. I don't know about you, but I'm really tired. Too tired to argue with you right now.''

''All right, I'll let it go for today. But we're going to talk, Megan, and we're going to do it real soon.''

Though she heard the determination in his voice, Megan was so relieved to have gained a reprieve, however temporary, that she gave it little thought. Grabbing the coffeepot, she turned back to him and offered a tentative smile.

''Ready for a refill?''

He eyed her sternly for several long moments, making her heart flutter nervously. Then, with a wry twist of his lips, he held out his mug.

''Sure. I'm still about a quart low.''

''I can take Matthew upstairs and change his diaper while you finish eating. Then we can head over to the hospital so you can pick up your car.''

Again, he gave her a long, studied look, making her shift from one foot to the other. Finally, he held out the baby with a muttered ''Whatever you say.''

As it turned out, Jake drove Megan and Matthew to the pharmacy first, waiting in the car with the increasingly cranky baby while she had the prescription filled. She gave Matthew a dose of the antibiotic as soon as she returned to the car, along with a few drops of the acetaminophen she'd also bought. Then Jake drove on to the hospital.

Neither of them had much to say. Jake seemed content to bide his time in acquiescence to her wishes. And Megan knew that keeping her mouth shut was the best way to avoid venturing into dangerous territory.

Thankfully, the rhythm of the moving vehicle settled the baby once again. As they pulled up alongside Jake's car and parked, Megan risked a glance at him.

"Thanks, again. For everything," she said.

"I'm glad I could help out." He hesitated a moment, then added, "Are we still on for Thursday night, or would you rather wait until another evening to get together?"

"Thursday should still be good," she replied, reminded of the previously scheduled meeting of the drug and alcohol abuse task force. "I think I'll call Steven, though, and suggest that we meet at my house instead of his. I was going to ask Jilly to baby-sit, and I'll still have her come over to keep an eye on Matthew, but I'd just as soon stay close by myself."

"Sounds like a good idea to me. Six-thirty Thursday at your house, then?"

"Yes."

"I'll be there." He flashed a sexy grin, taking her by surprise and making her tummy turn a somersault. Then he opened the car door as Matthew's whimpers escalated into ear-piercing shrieks. "Take care, Megan."

"You, too, Jake."

Her focus on Matthew once again, she slid over the

gearshift and wasted no time starting the car. With a last wave at Jake, she shifted into gear and drove out of the lot.

"Oh, baby, we're going straight home," she promised, glancing at Matthew's red, tear-stained face in the rearview mirror. "You'll feel better once we're there. I promise. We can both take a nice, long nap...."

Probably wishful thinking, Megan mused, but hope was a good thing to have.

Where Jake is concerned, too, a little voice whispered in the back of her mind.

Just as she had done earlier in the kitchen, Megan gave her head a firm, negative shake as she guided her car toward home. She might not be able to avoid talking to Jake about the past, but she didn't have to let whatever he had to say interfere with her common sense.

What she had needed from him, he hadn't been able to give her. And while he'd changed a lot in the time they had been apart, she knew better than to believe he had changed enough for her to trust him with her heart ever again.

Chapter Twelve

The Thursday night drug and alcohol task force meeting was a big success, at least as far as Jake was concerned.

Megan hosted the group that included Steven Barns, a couple of other teachers and the football coach, two members of the school board, one of whom was a local physician, and the president of the school's PTA.

All had agreed that they had a lot of hard work ahead of them to fight the growing problems of drug and alcohol abuse among the students at Serenity High School. Their top priority had to be enlisting the cooperation of the parents, many of whom seemed to have abdicated their responsibility for their teenage sons and daughters.

To that end, there would be several programs presented to students, teachers and parents alike at the start of the school year in August, including one by the hospital trauma team and another by the police department. And the enforcement of zero tolerance, even for the star quarterback, should the situation arise, was also deemed necessary.

By nine o'clock, the meeting was over and the last of the attendees were saying good-night to Megan. In what he hoped wouldn't seem like an obvious attempt to be the last to leave, Jake busied himself clearing up the paper plates and cups used to serve the iced tea, coffee and homemade cookies Megan had provided.

When Steven Barns finally headed toward the front door, Jake heaved a quiet sigh of relief. Now all he had to do was run upstairs where Jilly was looking after Matthew and tell her she was free to go, as well. Then he would have Megan all to himself, at last.

Jake had tried to talk to her on Tuesday morning. He had tried to tell her that seeing her at the hospital, clutching Matthew in her arms, on her own and so obviously afraid, he'd been hit by the true depth of the anguish she must have experienced when Will died. And that in the long, lonely hours before dawn, when he'd walked the floor with Matthew, he had finally understood, clearly and completely, just how much he'd let her down after their son was born.

Megan had put him off, though, and he had held back, as he had so many other times since he'd returned to Serenity. He couldn't let the words go unsaid any longer, though—words of regret and bitter remorse, words of apology that would hardly make up for what he'd done, and the most difficult words of all, asking for the forgiveness he didn't deserve but wanted, *needed,* more than anything.

Jake found Jilly curled up in the upholstered chair he had moved from Megan's bedroom to the nursery earlier in the evening, reading by the pale light from the lamp on the nightstand. Matthew, obviously feeling better thanks to the antibiotic the emergency room doctor had prescribed, slept peacefully in his crib.

Pausing in the doorway, Jake used the few moments it took for her to realize he was there to look for some sign, *any* sign, that she was more than just the baby-sitter. Matthew could have gotten his blue eyes and blond hair from her, but Jake had yet to detect a more striking resemblance between them. And he had yet to come across a paper trail linking her to the baby.

So far, none of the hospitals he'd contacted had had a patient in their maternity ward during the time period when Matthew could have been born who even vaguely resembled her.

There was something about the way she held Matthew, though, something about the expression on her face when she first laid eyes on him after an absence, and something about the eager way the baby always went to her that continued to fuel his suspicions.

"Hey, Jilly, how's it going?" he asked after a last moment's hesitation.

Startled, she looked up at him, then smiled uncertainly as she shifted in the chair and sat up straight.

"Fine, Chief Cahill. Everything's just fine," she replied.

"I just wanted to let you know that the meeting is over. You're free to go anytime."

"Oh...okay."

She folded over a page in her book to mark her place and stood slowly, slinging the strap of her purse over her shoulder. Running a hand through her silky hair, she turned and gazed at Matthew, sleeping soundly in the crib, hesitated, then with a wry glance at Jake, walked over, smoothed a hand over the baby's downy head and whispered something Jake couldn't hear.

"Just saying good night," she explained, her eyes not quite meeting his as she moved away from the crib a moment later.

"You've gotten kind of attached to him, haven't you?" Jake asked, watching her intently.

Jilly shrugged noncommittally, slipping past him through the doorway.

"He's such a sweet baby. How could I not?"

"How, indeed?" he murmured as he followed her down the stairs.

Megan met them in the entryway, a grateful smile tugging at the corners of her mouth.

"There you are, Jake. And, Jilly, I was just coming up to get you. Thanks for looking after Matthew for me."

"It was no trouble at all, Mrs. Cahill. I enjoyed staying with him this evening."

"Here's a little something for you." Megan pressed a folded twenty-dollar bill into the younger woman's hand.

"Oh, no, I can't take money from you," Jilly protested, an oddly discomfited look on her face.

"It's nothing, Jilly, compared to all the help you've been to me over the past ten days. Take your friends out to lunch on me one afternoon."

"But I've wanted to help out. I've wanted..."

As if catching herself before she said more than she intended, Jilly clutched the twenty-dollar bill in her hand, stared at the floor for a long moment, then looked back at Megan and smiled slightly.

"Thanks," she murmured. "Thanks a lot."

Frowning, Jake watched as Megan gave Jilly a hug, then opened the front door and waved the young woman off with a promise to call if she needed her help again the following day.

He was tempted to say something about his suspicions to Megan right then and there. But he had other things he needed to say first. While he could easily broach the subject of Jilly Maitland's possible relationship to Matthew another time, he doubted he'd have as good a chance to talk to Megan about the past as he felt he had that night.

The success of their meeting had left her looking relaxed and happy, and he meant to use her mellow mood to his advantage.

With the door still partly open, Megan glanced at him.

"I guess you'll be going, too," she said. "Thanks again for helping with the cleanup." She gestured vaguely toward the kitchen as she looked away again.

Jake couldn't tell from her expression whether she wanted him to leave or not. She hadn't opened the door wide enough so he could walk out, but neither had she closed it all the way. Taking matters into his own hands, he reached around her and gently pushed the door shut, then took her by the arm when she flashed him a puzzled glance.

"Come and sit down with me. There are a few things we need to talk about."

She resisted for a moment, her arm tensing under his hand, then allowed him to turn her toward the living room. More than likely, she assumed he had something to tell her about Matthew's mother, he thought, glimpsing the anxious look on her face as he led her to the sofa and gently pulled her down beside him.

"You've found her, haven't you?" she asked in a strained voice, her pale gray eyes filled with trepidation. "You've found Matthew's mother."

"No, I haven't," he answered matter-of-factly.

"Then what is it? What's wrong?" She shot a worried glance toward the staircase, ready to leap up if necessary. "The baby's all right, isn't he?"

"He's fine. Sleeping like a baby," Jake quipped, offering her what he hoped was a reassuring smile.

Megan wasn't buying into it, though. When she met his gaze again, she eyed him warily, obviously still ready to make a fast getaway.

"So, what is it that we need to talk about, then?"

Jake had let go of her arm when they sat on the sofa. Now he took one of her hands in his, holding on to it firmly when she tried to pull away.

"I'm not sure where to begin," he admitted. "Maybe with the other night when I saw you walk into the emergency room with Matthew. I never really knew until then exactly what you must have gone through the night Will died...."

"I'd rather not discuss Will with you, Jake," Megan cut in, trying to free her hand from his as she lowered her gaze. "Every time we do, we only end up hurting each other. What happened...happened. There's no changing it, no matter how often we go over it."

"I know that. God, how I know that." Jake, too, looked away, though he continued to grip her hand, afraid that if he let her go, he would never get another chance to talk to her like this again. "Just as I finally know how much I let you down, not only when you had to go with Will alone to the emergency room, but before that, and especially, afterward.

"I should have been there for you and for our son. I should have put both of you first in my life. You were my wife and Will was my son, and I lost you both because I didn't realize how much the two of you meant to me until it was way too late.

"For that, I am so sorry, Megan. So very, very sorry..." His voice catching, Jake blinked hard as tears of remorse stung his eyes.

Beside him, Megan no longer fought to free herself from his hold. Instead, she clung to him, cupping his hand in both of hers.

"What happened with Will wasn't your fault, Jake," she stated kindly, making an obvious attempt to set his mind at ease. "As you told me when he started running a fever, babies get sick all the time, and like Matthew, they almost always get better within a day or two. You couldn't miss work every time our son had a sniffle and expect to keep your job.''

"But he didn't just have a sniffle.''

"We didn't know that at the time,'' she said, her tone taking on a pragmatic edge.

"He'd never been that sick before, though, and you were so worried about him.''

"But I chose to believe the pediatrician knew what he was saying. He told me to give the medication a chance to work, and that's what I did.''

Hearing the sudden tension in Megan's voice, Jake shifted on the sofa and put his arms around her. She leaned against him willingly, her head tucked under his chin, her dark curls soft against the edge of his jaw, and uttered an audible sigh.

"What else could you have done?'' he asked softly.

"I could have listened to my own intuition a lot sooner. I *knew* something was really, really wrong with Will, and I *knew* the medication wasn't helping. I should have taken him to the hospital hours earlier than I did. If I had, he might still be alive.''

"It wasn't your fault that Will died, either, Megan. It *wasn't*,'' Jake soothed as she clung to him, one sob, then another shuddering through her.

His own tears fell then, too, not for himself but for her, and the horrible burden she had carried since they'd lost their son. He had been so sure that she blamed him for Will's death. He had never imagined that she'd actually blamed herself.

"You did the best you could, on your own, in a

bad situation. I can't say I would have done any differently if I'd been there with you. But at least you wouldn't have had to make so many decisions by yourself. You didn't deserve to be alone then, Megan. And you didn't deserve to be alone after Will died. You wouldn't have been, either, if I'd been man enough to face up to how gravely I let you down from the very beginning.

"It hurt so much, though, to see you look at me with all that anguish in your eyes, and to know that I had never been the kind of husband or the kind of father I should have been, could have been...."

"Oh, Jake, I wanted you there with me, needed you there...." she said, her voice thick with the tears she still shed. "But I never blamed you for Will's death, and I never, ever meant to make you feel guilty."

"You had every right, though."

"No, I didn't. Not when it happened, and certainly not afterward. But I was just too tied up with my own grief and my own guilt to realize how much I was making you suffer, too."

Jake wanted to argue with her on that point, but he knew it wouldn't do any good just then. The pain he had lived with day in and day out the past three years had been all his doing. Nothing she said would ever convince him otherwise.

He didn't want her to feel responsible in any way. But he wasn't sure exactly how to take that burden from her. He would find a way, though. Very soon, he would find a way to help her let go of the guilt she had no reason to bear.

"I'm sorry, Megan," he murmured, brushing his

lips against her curls. "More sorry than you'll ever know for the way things turned out between us."

"Me, too, Jake." She eased back in his arms and looked up at him, her face wet with tears. "I made so many mistakes."

"No, Meg..."

"Yes...*yes.*" Meeting his gaze steadily, she put a hand on his cheek, willing him to let her share the blame.

"No," he muttered, then bent his head until his mouth was just a breath away from hers. "*No,*" he repeated yet again.

Before she could argue with him any further, he kissed her as he had wanted to kiss her so many times in the past few days. To his surprise, she didn't pull away. Instead, she opened her mouth to him, kissing him back.

Tightening his hold on her, Jake accepted her invitation with a low groan that spoke of needs all too long denied.

Chapter Thirteen

Megan tried to tell herself that she was responding to Jake's kiss because, once again, he'd taken her by surprise when she was most vulnerable. But deep in her heart she knew better as she angled her head just so, threaded her fingers through his dark, shaggy hair and opened her mouth to him in eager invitation.

Not a day had gone by since she'd left him that she hadn't missed the intimacy they had once shared. Only Jake had been able to stir the passion in her soul—a passion always edged with wonder and joy. Only the masterful touch of his hands on her, the tempting, teasing, oh-so-possessive way he used his lips, his teeth, his tongue, could bring her the pleasure that had so often been almost too intense to bear.

She had worked hard over the past three years to deny the longing, to bury it beneath the anger, the bitterness and the pain of his emotional abandonment. And she would have succeeded, could have succeeded, if only she hadn't needed his help finding Matthew's mother.

By keeping her distance from Jake, by shutting him out of her life, she had been able to convince herself that they couldn't have been *that* good together. Otherwise, they wouldn't have drifted so far apart.

But spending time with him over the past two weeks had triggered memories too powerful for her to ignore. Her willpower had been whittled away. She felt weak when she breathed in his all-too-familiar scent, when she watched the way he held the baby or saw the unguarded look in his eyes when he glanced her way. His voice deepened and softened, taking on a blissful buoyancy, when he spoke to her. When she'd danced with him at the church picnic, the brush of his lips on her cheek had her longing for more.

And then, tonight, when he talked about Will and the blame he had put upon himself, Megan had realized, perhaps for the first time, how much their son's death had affected him, too. He hadn't been able to reveal his deepest feelings all those years ago—hadn't been able to let his own anger, his pain and his grief show. His feelings had been as anguished as hers, but he had kept them hidden from her, just as she had kept *her* feelings hidden from him. They had been so mired in their own guilt that they had turned away from each other.

Listening to Jake that evening, Megan had finally been able to see that she'd been as responsible as he, driving him away with the silent condemnation she had meant for herself, but which he'd believed to be aimed at *him.*

No wonder he had found every excuse he could to stay out of her way. How grateful he must have been to have a job that took him out of her orbit for days, even weeks, at a time. Throwing himself into his work must have been the only thing that kept him going through those dark and lonely days.

As if suddenly unsure about what he was doing, what *they* were doing, Jake raised his head, breaking off their kiss.

"Megan...?" he murmured, a questioning look in his eyes as he brushed the back of his fingers against her cheek in the gentlest of touches.

"Yes, Jake?"

She reached up and cradled the side of his face with her hand, rubbing the pad of her thumb along his cheekbone, wiping away the dampness left there by his tears.

"I want you. I want you so much. All these years..."

He hesitated. Then, closing his eyes, he leaned his forehead against hers. "All these years I've never stopped wanting you."

"I want you, too, Jake," she whispered.

At her words, the tension she had sensed in him seemed to ease.

"You do?"

"Yes." Sitting back, she took his hand in hers, then stood slowly, tugging on his arm. "Come upstairs with me...please."

A look of surprise flashed in Jake's eyes, followed almost at once by a flurry of other emotions—relief, gratitude and, finally, jubilation as he scooped her into his arms and headed for the staircase, his strides long and sure and steady.

As Megan clung to him, her arms around his neck, she experienced one small, silent moment of uncertainty. She wanted to make love with Jake tonight— wanted it as much as she had ever wanted anything. But only this one time, she temporized.

One time to heal the hurt they had caused themselves and each other. One time to soothe away the worst of the grief and the guilt they had lived with since their son's death.

Then Jake could return to Dallas and his job with the bureau, and she could get on as best she could with the life she had made for herself in Serenity.

"Should we check on the baby?" he asked, pausing outside Matthew's room.

From the doorway, elevated as she was in Jake's arms, and thanks to the soft glow of the lamp on the nightstand, Megan could see the baby sleeping peacefully in his crib.

"He'll let us know if he needs anything," she said.

"Yes, he most certainly will." Chuckling softly, Jake moved on to her bedroom.

He carried her across the room, then set her on her feet beside the bed. Seeming suddenly hesitant in the darkness, he traced a hand over her hair, smoothing an errant curl away from her face.

Touched by how vulnerable he must be feeling, Megan put her hands on either side of his face and pulled him close for a kiss deep enough to reassure him that her intentions hadn't changed.

Arms around her, he drew her into his embrace and kissed her back with equal fervor.

Despite all the time they had been apart, Megan wasn't in any rush to satisfy her needs. To her gratification, neither, it seemed, was Jake. For several long, luscious minutes he contented himself with kissing her, tasting, then tempting her to taste back in ways that stole her breath away.

Her nipples rubbed against the silky fabric of her bra, tight and hard as tiny pebbles. She wondered whether Jake could feel them through the shirt he wore, just as she could feel the rigid length of him, still covered by his jeans, pressing boldly against her belly.

How quickly, and how easily, they could still excite each other...

Releasing her mouth, Jake bent his head and set to work on the curve of her ear, using his tongue to torment her in yet another way. Finally, he cupped her breasts in his hands and teased her nipples with his thumbs.

Not to be outdone despite the sudden weakness in her knees, Megan slipped a hand between their bodies and rubbed her palm over him, up, then down, and up again until he caught her hand in his and pulled it away.

"You know that makes me crazy," he growled, then gently nipped the side of her neck, sending a shiver racing down her spine.

"And you know *that* makes *me* crazy," she answered back, bracing her hands on his shoulders to hold herself steady. Tilting her head to one side, she gave him easier access to the spot he licked, then nipped again.

"This, too…" A hint of laughter in his voice, he leisurely ran his free hand up her jeans-clad thighs and stroked her between her legs with just enough pressure to make her writhe against his fingers.

Maybe taking it slow wasn't such a good idea, after all, she thought, her breath escaping in a gasp of pleasure as she rose up on her toes to follow the sudden retreat of his touch.

"Please, Jake," she murmured, resting her forehead on his shoulder.

"I want to watch you undress," he said. Stepping away from her, he switched on the lamp on the nightstand, then stood with his hands on his hips, his gaze on her intent. "But slowly…"

Megan wanted to rip off her clothes and throw herself at him. Wanted to unzip his jeans, pull him free and climb onto him where he stood, her legs wrapped around his waist. Wanted to feel the length of him inside her, pulsing hard with desire. She was hot and wet and ready for the release only he could give her.

Instead, she pulled the hem of her T-shirt from the waistband of her jeans with shaking hands, then eased it up and over her head. Next, she kicked off her sandals, one at a time, unfastened her jeans and slowly eased them down her legs.

His eyes shadowed, Jake stood motionless, watching her, his fascination obvious.

With a new and exciting sense of power, Megan ran her fingers through her dark curls, arching her back slightly, letting Jake look his fill at her bra-andpantie-clad body. As if regretting the instructions he'd given her, he started to reach for her, but she took a step back, holding up a warning hand.

A wry smile twitching at his lips, Jake lowered his hands to his sides again.

Wordlessly, Megan smiled, too, then reached around to unclasp her bra. She had every intention of preening again before discarding her panties, but Jake gave her no chance. Closing the distance between them, he took the bra from her and tossed it aside, grabbed hold of her panties, slipped them off, then tumbled her onto the bed with a masculine growl that sent another shiver down her spine.

"Hey, no fair," she laughed, tugging at his shirt. "I want to watch you undress, too."

"Next time," he muttered, easing away from her just long enough to tear off his clothes before he pulled her under him again.

Next time, Megan thought. *Yes, next time…*

Her vow of *once only* broken as quickly as it had been made, she threaded her fingers through Jake's hair and pulled him close, ready for another of his searing kisses.

As if he could wait no longer, he levered himself between her legs, shoved an arm under the small of her back and lifted her into his thrust. She spread herself wide, taking him deep inside her, then wrapped her legs around his hips and arched her back, dragging him as close to her core as she could.

"I can't…can't hold back," he muttered, his breathing raspy as he pumped into her hard and fast.

In answer, Megan called his name in a voice she

barely recognized as her own, a shattering release sending shock waves through her with such force she couldn't seem to catch her breath. Swept along on the tide of her pleasure, Jake, too, reached a powerful climax, rearing back as he poured himself into her with a muffled shout of ecstasy.

For a long time afterward, they lay entwined together, gasping as they tried to catch their breath. Finally, reluctantly, Jake started to roll off her, but a trembling Megan clung to him, turning onto her side, as well, unwilling, just yet, to break the intimate bond created by their mating.

"Are you all right?" he asked, smoothing a hand over her hair.

Unable to speak, she nodded her head against his chest, curling as close to his warmth as she could. Then, to her surprise and utter dismay, she began to cry quietly.

"Megan? What is it?" His voice filled with concern, Jake bent to feather a kiss along the edge of her jaw.

"Just hold me, please," she managed to say.

"For as long as you want," he vowed.

To Megan's relief, her tears stopped almost as soon as they'd started. She couldn't say exactly what had brought them on. No doubt the surfeit of emotions she'd experienced since she and Jake first sat down on the sofa had had a lot to do with it, though.

Under normal circumstances, she would have been embarrassed by such a show of emotion, but not tonight. Tonight the tears she had shed, not once but twice, had a cathartic effect on her. Suddenly, she felt as if a great weight had been lifted from her shoulders. For the first time since losing Will, she was at peace with herself and with Jake, and she wanted the moment to last forever.

Matthew had other ideas, of course. At almost the same instant, Megan and Jake heard the first little whimpers signaling the baby's need for a fresh diaper and a last bottle of formula before settling down for the rest of the night.

"I'll get him," Jake offered, easing away from her.

"There's a bottle in the refrigerator." Megan, too, sat up and ran a hand through her hair. "Run down and pop it in the bottle warmer while I change his diaper."

As Jake pulled on his jeans, she crossed to the closet, not the least bit embarrassed by her nakedness, grabbed a short royal-blue silk robe, then hurried into the baby's room.

She had just finished fastening Matthew's sleeper over a fresh diaper when Jake joined her with the warm bottle.

"Let's take him back to bed with us," he said, slipping an arm around her shoulders.

"Okay," Megan agreed with a shy smile.

On her bed, Jake sat propped against the headboard with their pillows behind his back, and she settled against his chest. As Matthew sucked eagerly at the bottle, Jake put his arms around them both, holding them in a protective embrace.

Neither of them spoke, but their silence, broken only by the sound of the baby gulping down his formula, was utterly peaceful. Megan could also feel the steady beat of Jake's heart against her cheek, and that added to her sense of security.

They were a family again—patched together temporarily at best, of course, but still a family. She allowed herself to savor the wonder and joy of the moment to the fullest.

When Matthew had finished his bottle and had been duly burped, Jake took him back to his crib. By the time he returned to the bedroom, Megan had discarded her robe and lay back on the pillows, an inviting smile lingering at the corners of her mouth.

Jake barely paused before he shucked his jeans and stretched out beside her again. One glimpse at him had assured Megan he was as ready for her as she was for him.

"Want to turn off the lamp?" she asked.

"No." Taking her wrists in one of his hands, he stretched her arms over her head.

"But you know I can't sleep with the light on," she pouted prettily as she slid down next to him and arched her hips.

"Oh, not to worry. It's going to be a while before you're ready to sleep."

"You sound awfully sure of that." She faked a yawn and closed her eyes.

"I am." With a rumble of laughter, he dipped his head and burrowed his lips between her legs, making her breath catch in her throat and her eyes open wide.

"Jake…oh, *Jake*…"

Again, he laughed, and this time Megan felt it, as well as heard it, all the way to the center of her being.

Chapter Fourteen

Jake awoke in Megan's bed, holding her close in his arms, her naked body warm against his as they lay together, spoon-style. Opening his eyes slowly just as dawn began to chase away the night shadows in the unfamiliar room, he lay as still as he could, matching the rhythm of his breathing to hers.

He didn't want to disturb her sleep any sooner than absolutely necessary. A glance at the clock on the nightstand assured him Matthew would more than likely do the honors very soon, anyway, if he stuck to his usual schedule. In the meantime, Jake wanted to savor whatever moments of intimacy he had left with his ex-wife.

There was no telling how she would feel about the sudden, unexpected change their strained relationship had undergone the night before. For whatever reason, she had been as eager as he had been to make love. In fact, she had been the one to turn his meant-to-soothe kiss into something much more sexual in nature.

Not that he had objected in any way. But in the clear light of a new day, Megan might choose to chalk up her actions to a lapse in what she considered good, old-fashioned common sense. They were divorced, after all—had been for a while—and, as far as she was concerned, for a very good reason.

They had never really talked about Will's death the way they had last night, each revealing their sense of guilt as well as their remorse. Such a baring of one's soul often brought with it a momentary aberration in behavior.

Megan had been vulnerable last night, and he had known it. What if she chose to believe he'd taken advantage of her? Even though he didn't think that was true, trying to convince her otherwise would likely come across as self-serving.

While nothing could ever completely obliterate his grief over losing his son, Jake had experienced an odd sense of absolution after he and Megan had made love. When she opened her arms to him and held him close, welcoming him into her very soul, the burden of guilt he had carried with him for so long had finally lifted.

He didn't want their reconciliation to be only temporary. He had tasted redemption in Megan's arms. He had been given a reprieve, one he wasn't sure he deserved, but one he wanted to last far beyond this moment when she still allowed him to hold her close to his heart.

Unconsciously, Jake flexed the fingers of the hand he had splayed possessively over Megan's belly, and wondered if a new life was already growing deep inside her. His heart swelled with the tenderest of hopes as she stirred against him with a soft sigh, signaling that she was no longer quite so sound asleep. A few minutes later, she tensed in his arms as if realizing she wasn't alone in her bed.

As he held his breath, waiting for her to shove away from him, she relaxed against him, put a hand over his and sighed again, peacefully.

"Jake..." she murmured.

In answer, he nuzzled the back of her neck, his relief so great he didn't quite trust himself to speak yet.

"I thought I was dreaming."

"Is that good or bad?" he managed to ask, a tremor of lingering uncertainty in his voice.

She wasn't fully awake, he reminded himself. And when she was, there was a good chance she might not feel quite so kindly toward him.

"It's good that I wasn't *only* dreaming," she replied, shifting onto her back so that she could look up at him.

"I was afraid you'd think it was a mistake...our making love," he admitted, his eyes searching hers, trying to read how she really felt in their pale gray depths.

"No, not last night." Though her hand still covered his where it rested on her belly, she lowered her gaze.

''What about now?'' He tried to keep his tone light, but his gut constricted anxiously as he saw the way her mouth turned down in a frown.

''I don't know, Jake,'' she said, her confusion evident. Still, she lay close to him, her cheek against his chest, her breath a warm tickle on his bare skin. ''It's probably not—''

''A bad idea?'' he cut in before she had a chance to say the opposite.

''Oh, Jake…'' She met his gaze again, her smile edged with exasperation.

''Oh, Megan,'' he growled in return.

Before she could protest further, he rolled on top of her and pinned her down, letting her feel the hunger pulsing through his loins as he took her mouth in a deep, soulful kiss.

She hesitated an instant, then put her arms around him, holding him close, kissing him back as she shifted under him, fitting her soft, wet warmth to his rigid length.

As luck would have it, Matthew chose that moment to let them know he was ready to start the day, too. His lusty cries made both Jake and Megan smile as Jake raised his head.

''Should have known,'' he muttered, pressing a kiss on her forehead.

Rolling away from her, he swung his legs over the side of the bed, aware that he didn't really mind the interruption. Not when he had the thought of Megan's eager embrace to carry him through the day.

Whatever reservations she might have about the turn their relationship had taken, he was sure he could find a way to override them. She wanted him as much as he wanted her, and he could think of no better foundation on which they could build for the future— a future that suddenly looked much brighter than he would have ever believed possible.

"I'll have to fill a bottle," Megan said, taking the blue silk robe he offered her. "We used the last one I had in the refrigerator last night."

"I'll do diaper duty, then." Jake flashed a grin her way as he pulled on his jeans. "But only if you promise to put on a pot of coffee, too."

"Promise."

As Megan started past him toward the bedroom doorway, Jake caught her hand and pulled her into his arms for a last quick kiss. She kissed him back with a fervor that surprised him. Then, squeezing his hand, she shot him a shy smile as she finally stepped away.

They had definitely turned a corner, Jake thought, grabbing his shirt and slipping it on as he padded, barefoot, to the baby's room. Their lovemaking the night before hadn't been the final farewell he'd feared Megan might have intended it to be—a last sharing of their hearts and souls, to put closure to the past before they each went their separate ways. Rather, it had been the first step toward a new beginning together. One Megan seemed to want as much as he.

They had each changed a lot in the time they'd been apart. Megan was no longer the fearful, dependent young mother who had unconsciously frightened him. And he was no longer the carefree, reckless boy with skewed priorities who had abandoned her out of his own insecurity.

In fact, they had grown up at last. And miracle of miracles, it seemed that their love for each other had survived—the love that had first brought them together, and that he, for one, had found impossible to live without.

Jake lifted a squalling Matthew from his crib and settled him on the changing table.

"Hey, little guy, how are you doing this morning?" he asked as he unsnapped the baby's cotton knit sleeper.

Matthew rewarded him with a teary-eyed smile and a wave of his arms.

"Good, huh?" Jake continued as he replaced the dirty diaper with a fresh one. "Me, too. I'm doing real good myself. Now, how about we head downstairs and have some breakfast with our Megan?"

The baby cooed happily when Jake lifted him into his arms and held his solid weight against his chest. He obviously knew the routine, and as long as a warm bottle of formula awaited him at the end of their walk down the stairs, he'd be satisfied.

Megan had Matthew's bottle ready and the coffee brewing by the time Jake joined her in the kitchen. She also had the ingredients for a batch of his favorite pecan pancakes assembled on the counter.

"Can you stay for breakfast?" she asked with the same shy smile she'd offered him earlier.

"Wild horses couldn't drag me out of here until I've had some of your pancakes," he assured her, sitting in his usual chair by the table with Matthew and the bottle in hand.

Megan set a mug of coffee on the table where he could easily reach it, then crossed to the stove and poured small circles of pancake batter on the hot griddle. "Are you working today?" she asked.

"I'm scheduled for the morning shift, but I can change that if you need my help around here."

"Oh, no," she said. "I was just curious." She hesitated a moment, then added, "Have you had any ideas at all about Matthew's mother? About who she might be?"

"I've been giving it a lot of thought, but I haven't gotten a definite fix on any one person," he hedged, unwilling, just yet, to mention his suspicions about Jilly Maitland. Then, aware that Megan might have more of a reason to pose such a question than mere inquisitiveness, he asked, "What about you? Do *you* have any thoughts about who she might be?"

When Megan didn't answer immediately, Jake looked over at her. She was staring intently at the plate of pancakes she held in one hand, definitely mulling something over in her mind.

"No," she said at last, lifting her shoulders in a seemingly careless shrug. "Not really."

Jake had a feeling she wasn't being completely honest with him. She obviously had someone in mind despite her protest, and he wondered if it was the same someone he had pegged. He thought about pressing her further, but before he could, Matthew spit up all over the front of his shirt.

"Oh, yuck." Making a face, Megan set the pancakes on the table and took the baby from him so he could wipe off the messy glob.

By the time Jake finished with his shirt, she had Matthew tucked into the little slanted infant seat at the far end of the table, and the moment had passed to ask her about Jilly. Whatever thoughts had crossed her mind about the baby's mother, she didn't seem ready to share them yet, and Jake could see no reason to push her.

As for his suspicions, he decided it would be best to continue to keep them to himself, at least until he had a chance to make his calls to the remaining hospitals on his list.

With the baby gurgling contentedly, they enjoyed their breakfast in companionable silence. Megan seemed as hesitant as he to dispel the magic they'd made together by delving too deeply or too critically into the whys and wherefores of it.

In whatever way, and for whatever reason, they had found something they had each feared they'd lost forever, and hanging on to it was all that they wanted to do just then.

When they had finished eating, Jake offered to clear the table, tidy the kitchen and keep an eye on Matthew while Megan went upstairs to take a shower. She gratefully agreed to his suggestion, the seductive smile she tossed over her shoulder as she left the kitchen making him wish he could join her.

Once he was alone, he called the station to let Darcy Osgood know that he was running late. Much to his relief, there were no pressing matters needing his attention so far that morning. In fact, he could dawdle as long as he liked at Megan's house without putting anyone out. And he was tempted to do just that.

So far, Megan hadn't appeared to have any regrets about their lovemaking, but Jake was afraid to imagine the thoughts that might start going through her head once she was on her own again. He didn't want her to think, even for a moment, that she had made a mistake by letting him back into her life again in such an intimate way.

He wanted to make her believe that he would never let her down again, and he could only do that by being there for her, physically as well as emotionally, no matter what happened.

Unfortunately, he couldn't dog her tracks twenty-four hours a day, seven days a week, though. He had to trust that she would keep him in her heart and know that he was keeping her in his, just as he had every day they'd been apart.

"You're looking rather pensive," Megan said, joining him in the kitchen again as he finished loading their plates into the dishwasher.

"Hey, that was fast." Jake glanced at her in surprise and saw that she was dressed in white shorts and a bright red T-shirt. Her soft curls were still damp and her feet were bare, but otherwise, she looked ready for whatever the day had in store for her.

"Three-minute showers…they come with the territory," she replied with a quick grin.

"You could have taken your time this morning."

"I thought maybe you'd want to stop home before you went to the station."

"I called in. All's quiet there so I'm not in any hurry. Unless you're ready to get rid of me," he added.

"Not really..." she began, then paused as the doorbell rang.

Frowning, she glanced at the clock above the refrigerator. It was only ten past eight.

"Now, who could that be?" she wondered, starting toward the living room.

"Jilly Maitland, perhaps?" Jake guessed, though not loud enough for Megan to hear.

Lifting Matthew from his seat, he followed after her, halting a few steps behind her as she opened the front door.

"Jilly...hi..." Megan said, making an effort—or so it seemed to Jake—to sound welcoming.

"Hi, Mrs. Cahill. I was up early and I thought I'd stop by and see if you needed any help with Matthew today," she replied, a hopeful note in her voice.

As he moved forward, Jake saw that Matthew was looking toward the open doorway and waving his arms excitedly.

"Hi, Jilly," he said, pausing next to Megan.

"Um, Chief Cahill, hi," she replied, eyeing him nervously. Then, as if she'd suddenly realized why he was at Megan's house so early in the morning, his face beard-shadowed, his shaggy hair tousled, his shirttails hanging out and his feet bare, she blushed and quickly looked away. "Oh, gosh, I'm *so* sorry...."

"Jilly, it's okay," Megan assured her, taking her

hand and drawing her into the house. "Jake was just getting ready to leave."

She gave him a pointed look as she took the baby from him.

"Yeah, I was," he said none too enthusiastically, though he did have those calls to make. "I'll just run upstairs to the bedroom and get my boots," he added, then grinned when he saw Megan blush almost as deeply as Jilly, who giggled self-consciously.

By the time he came downstairs again, shirt tucked into his jeans and wearing his boots, Megan was back in the kitchen with Jilly, making another batch of pancakes while the young woman danced around the table with Matthew balanced on her hip.

"They'll be here tomorrow afternoon...." Jilly was saying, obviously in answer to a question Megan had asked, and apparently referring to her parents.

"I'm sure you'll be glad to have them home again," Megan said.

"I guess." Jilly shrugged, then caught sight of Jake standing in the doorway and shifted her gaze away.

"I'm leaving," Jake announced, walking over to Megan and putting his arm around her.

She glanced up at him in surprise and he took the opportunity to plant a smacking kiss on her totally luscious lips.

"See you later," he advised, giving her shoulder a squeeze.

"Later?" She shot him a puzzled look.

"Yeah, later. If Jilly doesn't mind baby-sitting tonight, I thought maybe we could have dinner at the Veranda."

"I don't mind at all," Jilly said.

"The Veranda?" Megan still looked confused.

"Say about six?"

"Okay…"

"See you then. And, Jilly, thanks a lot."

"No problem, Chief Cahill."

Smiling with satisfaction, Jake left the two women standing in the kitchen. Jilly may have cut his morning with Megan short, but she was going to let him have the evening in return. And in the meantime…

His smile fading, Jake headed home for a shower and a change of clothes. Then he was going to the station, where he would try to find out who Matthew's mother was, once and for all.

Not that he really wanted to. He was in no hurry to disturb the still all-too-tentative peace he'd begun to make with Megan. And there was a chance that's exactly what finding the baby's mother would do.

Without Matthew to draw them together, Megan might find excuses to return to her solitary life—unless he had time to make himself a necessary part of that life first. He had made a reasonable start already, but their mutual concern for Matthew's well-being was a tie he was hesitant to break.

Once the baby was reunited with his mother, Jake wouldn't have a reason to see Megan on a daily basis. And by being the one to make it necessary for her to give up the child she had welcomed into her heart as her own, he would also be setting himself up for a certain amount of blame, no matter how unintentionally meant.

Granted, Megan had asked him to find Matthew's

mother. But she could still hold him accountable for the loss she would surely suffer when the baby was no longer in her care.

Jake could tell himself that he was only doing his job for the good of all concerned, and Megan would understand his motives, as well. But there was no guarantee she would act accordingly if her heart broke from the loss of another child.

It would be his fault this time, no matter what, and if she couldn't forgive him, he would lose her all over again.

Still, what other choice did he have?

Chapter Fifteen

With Jilly ready, willing and able to keep Matthew entertained that Friday morning, Megan first tried to work on the high school history curriculum she had barely glanced at the past couple of weeks. She couldn't seem to muster the concentration necessary to do the job justice, however. Thoughts of Jake, and also Jilly, kept flitting through her mind, distracting her at every turn.

Eventually she put away her books and papers, ate the lunch Jilly conscientiously prepared for them, then went out to the backyard to prune the roses planted around the gazebo. She had to decide what to do about Jake, *and* about Jilly, and she had found there was no better place to sort through her alternatives than out in the garden.

With the sun warm on her shoulders and the slight

breeze that rustled through the trees ruffling her curls, Megan worked her way from one side of the gazebo to the other, snipping off past-their-prime rose blossoms, then carefully cutting back dead wood as her thoughts whirled.

She knew that eventually she would end up regretting the wanton way in which she'd made love with Jake. But just then, the memory of how he'd kissed her, touched her, taken possession of her, had her longing, all over again, for the pleasure she'd experienced in his arms.

When she looked ahead to her date with him that evening, it wasn't the thought of sitting across the table from him, having dinner at the Veranda that made her heart beat a little faster in anticipation. It was the thought of the time they would share afterward, when they came back to the house, and she invited him to stay the night.

However, she shouldn't act as if they had a future together. Shouldn't even *think* that it was possible.

More than anything, their lovemaking had been the means by which they'd finally healed past wounds. By coming together as they had, their passion burning hot and fierce, they had finally absolved themselves, and each other, of blame for their son's death—blame neither of them had ever deserved. In each other's arms, they had found the closure they had so long been denied.

Welcoming Jake into her bed tonight would have nothing to do with the past. Yet Megan still couldn't believe they had any chance of a future together.

Jake might say that he was content living in Serenity, working as a small-town chief of police, but he'd been there only a year. Surely, given a little more time, he would realize how bored he really was. Then he'd go back to work for Bobby Fuentes, and she'd be right where she'd been three years ago—alone in a big city, waiting for her husband to find time for her between undercover cases.

Megan couldn't live that way again. She wouldn't. Not after the two years she'd spent in Serenity. She deserved better than playing second fiddle to the demands of her husband's career. She wanted a partner she could count on, day in and day out. A man she could not only trust to be available for her when she needed him most, but who would also *want* to be there for her whether it was convenient or not.

Better to leave well enough alone than to risk putting herself into an impossible situation—as she could have so carelessly done last night. Thank goodness a check of the calendar had assured she wasn't likely to have gotten pregnant.

Keeping Jake at arm's length from now on was the only smart thing to do, she warned herself sternly. But for all the grief she knew she would be opening herself up to, she could no more have called and canceled their date than she could have flown to the moon.

Nor would she be able to say good-night to him at her front door—mistake that it would surely prove to be. She wanted a little more time with him—needed it with something she feared was too close to desperation for her own good. And that time was quickly running out.

Once Matthew had been reunited with his mother, Jake wouldn't have anything more to keep him in Serenity. His duty done, he would be free to return to Dallas and the job Bobby Fuentes was holding open for him.

Matthew and his errant mother had brought her and Jake together again. But when the baby's mother came forward to claim him, Megan would have to let Jake go, along with the child she had grown to love as if he were her own.

Not an event she was anticipating with any great joy, Megan thought as she bagged up the debris from her pruning job. But one she had a duty to facilitate just as soon as she possibly could.

As she set the trash bag aside and climbed the steps of the gazebo, Megan's thoughts turned to Jilly. Sitting on one of the benches that lined the inside walls of the latticework, she tipped her head back and savored the feel of the cooler air inside the little building against her sun-warmed skin.

Since Monday night, when she had first begun to wonder if Jilly could be Matthew's mother, the thought had nagged almost constantly at the edges of her mind. Try as she might to dismiss the idea, it was making more and more sense to her—on some levels, at least.

Why else would a young woman, home from college for the summer, choose to spend so much of her time with an abandoned baby?

Granted, Jilly's parents had been gone most of the past two weeks, but she had several friends her own age, whose company she obviously enjoyed. And she hadn't wanted to be paid for her baby-sitting services, so she wasn't doing it to earn extra money.

Megan had also noticed how Jake had looked at Jilly the past couple of times their paths crossed. She had seen the thoughtful expression on his face as he'd eyed the young woman, and she had known, instinctively, that he had suspicions similar to hers even though he hadn't said anything about them yet.

And he wouldn't, she thought. Not until he had some proof. Accusing the beloved daughter of one of Serenity's most respected couples of abandoning her baby was something he would never do unless he knew, absolutely, that she was the guilty party.

Megan had kept her suspicions to herself for much the same reason. Why would Jilly abandon her baby when her own parents doted on her? Certainly they would have been happy to help her raise her child. They weren't lacking in financial resources, and from what Megan knew of them, they had always been kind and loving parents to their only child.

Wouldn't they be thrilled to welcome their first grandchild into their home?

Matthew might not have been born into the traditional family, but in this day and age, very few people considered that a cause for shame.

Of course, Jilly might think her parents would feel that way. And she might be afraid they'd force her to give up the baby for adoption. Though how that could be worse than what Jilly herself had done—abandoning her baby on someone's front porch, which constituted endangerment to a child—Megan couldn't imagine.

But she wasn't just any old someone, and Jilly hadn't really abandoned Matthew. Nor had she endangered him in any way, waiting, as she'd done, to make sure Megan found him before she fled.

If, in fact, Jilly *was* Matthew's mother—

"Mrs. Cahill?"

Startled by the voice of the very person so intently on her mind, Megan pushed off the bench and hurried to the gazebo doorway. The young woman stood at the foot of the steps, holding Matthew against her shoulder.

"Jilly? Is something wrong?" she asked.

"I thought maybe you'd lost track of time. It's almost five o'clock, and Chief Cahill said he would pick you up at six, didn't he?"

"Yes, I did, and yes, *he* did," Megan replied with a wry smile. "I'd better go in and take a shower."

"It's so nice out here. Do you mind if I sit in the gazebo with Matthew for a while?"

"Not at all. I'll let you know when I'm ready to leave."

Still thinking about Jilly, Megan took a quick shower, then dressed in a pale pink, thin-strapped, narrow-skirted sundress she'd bought in the spring but hadn't yet worn. She had a new pair of pale pink sandals that went with the dress, as well.

Should she mention her suspicions about the young woman to Jake at dinner? Probably, she admitted as she dabbed on a touch of lipstick. Any input into his investigation she could offer wouldn't hurt. If she was wrong about Jilly, only Jake would know of her suspicions. And if she was right...

Tugging her hairbrush through her tangled curls, still slightly damp from the shower, Megan frowned at her reflection in the mirror. If she was on the right track where Jilly was concerned, and if Jake agreed with her, they would have to confront the young woman without any further delay. Then, if Jilly was Matthew's mother, and she had a good reason for abandoning him, she would have to help her prove that she deserved to get him back.

Which meant Matthew would no longer have to be left in her care.

Megan had known from the first that Matthew wasn't her child, and she had tried hard not to pretend, even for a moment, that he ever would be. But that hadn't stopped her from loving him as if he were. And, perverse as it might seem to anyone else, that love was what had made her so determined to reunite him with his mother.

Because she loved Matthew, Megan could recognize his mother's love in the way he'd been cared for before he arrived on her front porch. And even in the way she'd left him—

The ringing of the doorbell drew Megan from her reverie. She set aside her hairbrush, grabbed her purse off the dresser on her way across the bedroom and ran lightly down the stairs.

Her heart fluttering in anticipation, she opened the door to find Jake waiting patiently, hands tucked in the side pockets of his casual khaki pants, the sleeves of his light blue cotton shirt rolled to his elbows. His eyes flashed with desire as he met her gaze, sending a shaft of heat zinging through her. Then he smiled slowly as he looked her up and down.

"You're looking lovely, Mrs. Cahill," he murmured, his words a soft caress she could almost feel against her skin.

"Thank you," she replied, reminded as he surely meant her to be, that they were a couple again.

Aware that she wasn't going to say or do anything that could spoil the time she was about to have with Jake, she blushed and looked away. Any serious discussion about Jilly Maitland would have to wait, at the very least, until tomorrow.

"Ready to go?" he asked.

"Just let me tell Jilly I'm leaving."

"Tell her we won't be late."

"Are you working the early shift tomorrow?"

"No, but we're having an early night tonight."

Jake's smile deepened suggestively, making Megan's knees go weak.

If she had any sense at all, she would say something to discourage him. But any sense she'd had where Jake Cahill was concerned had vanished when he'd taken her in his arms last night. And she wasn't about to coax it out of hiding until she absolutely, positively had no other choice.

Chapter Sixteen

Jake had spent the entire day looking forward to his date with Megan. She had rarely been far from his thoughts, even under normal circumstances. But now that there had been such a dramatic change in their relationship—a totally positive, thoroughly heartening change—he'd had a hard time concentrating on anything except how to keep the momentum going in a favorable direction.

He'd had every intention of making sure that having dinner together at the Veranda would set just the right mood for the rest of the evening. And standing on her front porch, waiting for her to let Jilly know she was leaving, he still did. Only it was going to be much more difficult, waiting, as he now was, for a call back from the admissions clerk at the small hospital in one of Chicago's more distant suburban neighborhoods.

Off and on all day, when he hadn't been busy taking statements from an elderly couple whose house had been robbed, refereeing a domestic squabble and making changes in the duty roster for the following week to accommodate two of his officers' court dates, Jake had continued to call the various Chicago area hospitals still on his list. A futile task, he'd decided by midafternoon when he'd had only a few hospitals left. But he refused to give up until he'd contacted every one.

Good thing, too, Jake thought. Late in the afternoon, he'd spoken to an admissions clerk who vaguely remembered that someone fitting Jilly's description had had a baby at her hospital during the time period he'd given. Unfortunately, the woman's computer had been temporarily out of service, so she hadn't been able to access the necessary records. She had promised to call him the following day, though, when her computer would be up and running once again.

"I'm ready if you are."

Megan joined Jake on the porch, a smile on her face as she pulled the door closed. He quickly set aside all thoughts of Jilly Maitland. Shifting out of investigator mode, he slipped an arm around his former wife and gave her a hug.

"More than ready," he replied.

"You should have come into the house," she said, walking down the steps with him, her arm slung around his waist companionably.

"It was so nice on your porch, I didn't mind waiting for you there, especially since I was stuck in the office most of the day."

"We can walk to the restaurant if you feel like it, then," Megan said. "We have enough time, don't we?"

"More than enough time," Jake assured her.

"Of course, we're going to have the neighbors talking," she commented, her voice laced with laughter as she waved at Mr. and Mrs. Bukowski, working in their yard just across the street.

"What do you mean *going to?*" he teased. "I think they've been at it since early this morning when they saw my car parked outside your house."

"Oh, yeah, right." Megan hugged him. "I forgot about that."

"I risk my reputation, and yours, I might add, and you've already forgotten about it?"

"Well, not really…"

She tipped her face up to smile at him, and he took the opportunity to plant a quick kiss on her luscious lips.

"Actually, not at all," she murmured before she looked away again.

"Hey, Chief Cahill, way to go, man," hooted a young, masculine voice.

A series of boisterous catcalls followed as a pickup truck bearing three teenage boys roared past.

"Slow it down," Jake shouted after them.

To his surprise, the driver pumped a fist out the window and complied.

"I wonder where they'll be partying tonight," Megan said.

"Hopefully at a house where the parents are home. But I've got officers patrolling the regular hangouts—the fairgrounds, the high school parking lot, the alley behind the businesses on Main Street and the cemetery."

"The cemetery?" Megan eyed him with disbelief.

"There hasn't been any vandalism yet so I've been able to keep it out of the local paper. But yes, there's a group of kids who occasionally congregate at the cemetery to drink beer and smoke pot."

"We've really got to get our task force up and running. And we should start thinking about sponsoring more organized activities for the high school students, too."

"Like weekend boot camps to keep them out of trouble," Jake muttered, only half teasingly.

Discussion of how best the task force could be utilized took them through dinner, much to Jake's relief. At their cozy table for two, over Caesar salad, grilled fish, a delicate mushroom risotto and steamed asparagus, they traded ideas, some workable, some not.

As the popular restaurant filled, several people stopped by, ostensibly to ask about Matthew. Jake suspected they were actually more interested in the sudden change in his relationship with his former wife. Megan didn't seem the least bit bothered by the attention, though, and so, neither was he. The more they were seen as a couple, a *happy* couple, the better.

As their meal progressed to dessert—a shared slice of chocolate pecan pie topped with homemade vanilla ice cream—Jake found himself wondering, perversely, why Megan hadn't asked him about the status of his search for Matthew's mother.

Maybe she assumed he no longer needed any prompting from her to relay whatever news he had. Maybe, too, she wanted tonight to be *their* night, much the same as he did.

They sorely needed this time together when they could not only focus on each other, but nurture, as well, the still tender emotions they had dared to reveal last night. Better not to let their conversation become too personal, especially out in public, while they were still finding their way back to each other.

Whatever Megan's reasons for not talking about Matthew or his mother, Jake was more grateful than he was curious. He couldn't see any harm in waiting until the following day—when he would know for sure if his lead panned out—to tell her what he suspected about Jilly.

"It's a good thing we walked here," Megan said as they left the restaurant just after eight o'clock.

Twilight had just begun to fall and a light breeze drifted through the leaves of the oak trees lining the sidewalk.

"Why do you say that?" Jake asked, putting his arm around her as he'd done on the walk there.

"Because I need to work off the calories in that pecan pie you insisted we share," she answered, leaning against him without the slightest hesitation.

"A few extra pounds wouldn't hurt you." He bent and kissed her on the cheek, lest she think he was criticizing her, then added, "But if you want a work-out tonight, I'll be happy to oblige."

As enjoyable as their dinner together had been, Jake knew there was no guarantee that Megan would allow him to spend the night. He didn't want to assume too much, too soon and frighten her into a full retreat. But at the same time, he didn't want her to think he would be satisfied leaving her at the front door with a platonic peck on the cheek.

"Oh, you will?" She glanced up at him with a sexy gleam in her pale gray eyes. "What, exactly, do you have in mind?"

"Something slow, but...intense." He grinned at her and winked. "Just wait and see. I promise you won't be disappointed."

"Well, if you say so...."

Jilly had just finished giving Matthew a bottle when they arrived at the house. Though still awake, the baby was drowsy-eyed and obviously ready for bed. Jilly offered to tuck him into his crib, and Megan nodded in agreement. A pensive look on her face, she then busied herself plumping up the sofa cushions while they waited for the young woman to join them in the living room once again.

"I can make some coffee," Megan offered in a half-hearted tone after a few moments had passed.

"Not for me," Jake said, catching her by the wrist and pulling her into his arms.

She came to him willingly enough, resting her head on his shoulder with a quiet sigh. But Jake sensed that she had something on her mind—something that concerned her deeply.

Not his presence there—otherwise she wouldn't be clinging to him so fiercely. What, then? he wondered. Matthew had seemed just fine, and so had Jilly. But since they'd entered the house, Megan's spirits had seemed to dip.

Could she possibly share his suspicions about Jilly? Could she be bracing herself to broach the subject with him?

At the sound of Jilly's footsteps on the stairs, Megan offered him a wry smile and eased out of his embrace. She took her purse from the end table where she'd set it, and dug a twenty-dollar bill out of her wallet.

"He was asleep by the time I put him down," Jilly advised, pausing in the living room doorway.

"Thanks for staying with him this evening," Megan said. Crossing to where the young woman stood, she slipped the money into her hand. "And for all your help today, too."

"You really don't have to pay me," Jilly protested as she had the other day. "I like spending time with Matthew, and I might not be able to the rest of the weekend. I have to drive to Dallas tomorrow morning to pick up my parents at the airport, and I'm not sure what they might have planned for Sunday. I can come over for a while on Monday, for sure, though. That is, if it's okay with you."

To Jake, she sounded unaccountably upset about the situation.

Megan, too, seemed to pick up on the young woman's odd tone of voice. She eyed her for a long moment, her gaze considering. Then she patted Jilly on the arm reassuringly.

"Not to worry," she said as she opened the front door. "I'll look forward to seeing you whenever you have time to stop by."

When they were alone again, Megan walked into Jake's outstretched arms. He thought she might say something about Jilly then, but she didn't. She held on to him wordlessly for several seconds, her face pressed against his chest. Then she took him by the hand and led him up to her bedroom.

She undressed, again without speaking, and so did he. As he'd promised, their lovemaking was slow and intense, and when they finally finished, one as sated as the other, she curled up against him trustingly until she slept.

Savoring the sweet-scented warmth of her body lying close to his, Jake stared at the shadows playing across the ceiling for a long time, willing away the dawn of a new day that could bring with it news that would devastate the woman he loved.

If Jilly was Matthew's mother, and her parents came to her rescue, as he suspected they would once they were apprised of the situation, Megan's services as foster mother would no longer be needed. Once again, she would be faced with the loss of a child she loved, and this time it *would* be his fault.

Sometime near dawn, wearied by his whirling thoughts, Jake slept, more deeply than he would have thought possible.

What seemed like only minutes later, but was really a few hours, he was brought sharply awake by the

sudden ringing of a telephone. Megan awoke, too, and
reached automatically for the handset on the nightstand beside the bed. She ran a hand through her tousled curls and offered a groggy hello, then shot him
a puzzled look as she listened to the voice on the
other end of the line.

"Yes, he's here," she said. "Hold on just a moment."

A thoughtful frown furrowing her forehead, she
held out the handset.

"For you. A Ms. Batson at the River Valley Hospital in River Valley, Illinois."

The admissions clerk he'd talked to yesterday afternoon, Jake realized. He had left several numbers
with her, including Megan's.

"Hello, Ms. Batson. This is Jake Cahill."

Megan held his gaze a moment. Then, hearing Matthew's first tentative cries, she slipped out of bed and
grabbed her robe.

"Chief Cahill, sorry to disturb you so early on a
Saturday morning, but our computers are up and running again, and I wanted to relay what I found in our
records before I got sidetracked."

"I appreciate your thoughtfulness, Ms. Batson."

"We had a maternity patient check into the hospital
in mid March by the name of Jillian Cates. She gave
birth to a son, Matthew. She wasn't a patient of any
of our staff physicians. She arrived here already in
labor, delivered her baby and checked out a day later.
She's been paying a small amount toward her hospital
bill each month ever since. I hope that helps."

"Yes, it helps a lot," Jake replied, glancing toward

the bedroom doorway. He could faintly hear Megan talking to the baby, who had stopped crying. "Thanks for calling."

After saying goodbye to Ms. Batson, Jake put in a call to the police station. At his request, one of the officers on duty quickly found the additional information he needed to be absolutely sure Jilly was Matthew's mother. Cates—the surname she'd used—turned out to be her mother's maiden name as well as her own middle name.

Jake also asked his officer to track down a copy of the baby's birth certificate, thanked him, then set aside the handset.

The last thing he wanted to do that sunny summer morning was tell Megan what he'd learned about Jilly Maitland. But he couldn't justify putting it off. He'd done what she'd asked—he had found Matthew's mother—and the sooner she knew it, the better. She was going to need as much time as he could give her to prepare herself emotionally for whatever happened next.

He only hoped she would let him help her, and in turn, help himself, because his life, too, would be emptier without Matthew in it.

Megan wasn't in Matthew's room, he quickly saw. Nor was she in the living room or the kitchen. Beginning to worry, Jake finally found her sitting on the front porch swing, wrapped in her robe, the baby nursing greedily from a bottle, cradled in her arms.

Slowly she turned to look at him as he moved toward her, and with a painful wrench, he realized, as she met his gaze, that there were tears staining her lovely face.

Chapter Seventeen

As Jake, dressed only in the khaki pants he'd worn the night before, stepped onto the porch and started toward her, Megan quickly looked away. Brushing ineffectually at her damp cheeks, she took a steadying breath.

She had hoped to have time to compose herself before he joined her, but it had been impossible. Instinctively, she had known that the woman calling Jake must have information for him concerning Matthew's mother. He wouldn't have left instructions to call at her house regarding anything else.

Of course, Ms. Batson's information might actually be that she had none. But that wouldn't let Megan off the hook. One way or another, she had to share her suspicions about Jilly with Jake, and she had to do it now.

She had been unforgivably selfish yesterday afternoon and again last night. Since she had first found Matthew on her front porch she had insisted that she wanted to see him be reunited with his mother. Yet she had purposely ignored all the signs that led to Jilly Maitland.

No matter how many times she'd told herself she could be mistaken, deep in her heart Megan had known why Jilly was spending so much time with the baby. She had seen it in the way the young woman looked at him when she held him in her arms. And she had heard the desperation in her voice last night when she'd said that she would have to spend most of the weekend with her parents.

She could have spoken up then, could have voiced her suspicions once and for all, and perhaps, if she was right about Jilly, put in motion the process by which Jilly could eventually reclaim her son. Instead, coward that she was, she had let Jilly leave so *she* could pretend, for one last night, that with Matthew sleeping in his crib and Jake holding her close in his arms all was right with *her* world.

"What's wrong?" Jake asked softly, sitting beside her on the porch swing.

Megan drew another steadying breath. But she was too ashamed of hiding what she'd suspected to make herself meet his gaze, and she didn't trust her voice enough to speak.

"Is Matthew okay?"

She nodded wordlessly, her grip on the baby tightening imperceptibly.

"What about you? Are you okay?"

The gentleness in his voice was her absolute undoing, and Megan gave her head a negative shake as a sob shook her shoulders.

"Oh, Meggie, don't cry," Jake soothed, putting an arm around her and drawing her close. "Everything's going to be all right. I promise."

"I...I've been so selfish," she said as she set aside the empty bottle, then dug futilely in the pocket of her robe for a tissue.

"In what way?" Pulling a clean handkerchief from the back pocket of his pants, Jake blotted her face with it as he would a child's.

"I think I know who Matthew's mother is, and I...I didn't say anything to you because I didn't want to spoil our time together last night."

"I've been fairly sure who Matthew's mother is the past few days myself. But I didn't want to say anything to you until I was absolutely sure for exactly the same reason," Jake admitted quietly. "Being here with you and Matthew the past couple of weeks has meant more to me than I can say. He brought us together again, and he's kept us together. It's been hard knowing that once I found his mother I wouldn't have a reason you'd accept to come here anymore."

And I assumed—still do, in fact—that once you'd done your job you'd decide to go back to Dallas, Megan thought, but didn't say.

Instead she murmured quietly, "You can come here anytime you want to, Jake, whether Matthew's here or not."

"That's good to know." He brushed a kiss against her curls, then added, "And believe me, I intend to hold you to it. We've healed a lot of old wounds the past couple of weeks, and we've found our way back to each other. I want for us to build on that foundation.''

Megan didn't doubt that Jake meant what he said just then. In time, though, as life in Serenity settled down to normal, he would be champing at the bit for something more thrilling than small-town life had to offer him.

They had each changed for the better since Matthew had come into their lives. But neither of them had changed completely. Jake had always thrived on the excitement of undercover work, and Megan believed he always would. As for her, she would rather be alone than trust again that he'd be able to put her wants and needs above the demands of his job.

''I take it you're certain now about the identity of Matthew's mother?'' she asked, seeking safety in a return to the starting point of their conversation.

''Yes,'' Jake admitted with obvious reluctance. ''The woman who called was able to verify that a young woman by the name of Jillian Cates gave birth to a son at River Valley Hospital outside Chicago in mid March. Cates is Jilly's mother's maiden name and her middle name.

''I have one of my officers tracking down Matthew's birth certificate, but even without it, I have enough to justify confronting Jilly. I'd like to wait, though, until her parents are back in town. There isn't a lot I can do over the weekend aside from arrest her for child endangerment and hold her in jail, and that seems a bit excessive under the circumstances. She made a mistake and I will have to arrest her and let the court decide her fate. But she did no real harm to Matthew, and she's certainly no danger to him or anyone else.''

"So, Jilly *is* Matthew's mother," Megan said. "I suspected as much, but I just couldn't quite believe she would abandon a baby she seems to love so much. I saw how she behaved with him, but I kept making excuses. And I kept running up against the same mental block. Why would she abandon her baby when she not only loves him, but has parents who dote on her, as well? Surely she has to know they would do whatever they could to help her?''

"She could have been afraid of disappointing them. She is their only child, and her father, for one, seems to have big plans for her future. She's awfully young, too, and she's lived a relatively sheltered life," Jake pointed out. "Whatever her motivation, we'll find out soon enough.''

"What are you going to do?" Megan asked.

"Talk to her first, and see what she has to say for herself, then talk to her parents. Although I hate dumping all this on them just as they're getting home today.''

"What if I talked to Jilly tomorrow?" she suggested, eyeing him thoughtfully as an idea came to mind. "I could invite her to come over in the afternoon, tell her what we've found out, and see what she has to say for herself. Then I could go with her to talk to her parents. I think it would probably be better for Jilly, and for them, if they found out about Matthew from her rather than from you." Aware that she was postponing the inevitable yet again, Megan turned her gaze back to Matthew. "Unless that would create a legal problem for you."

Jake hesitated only a moment, then gave her a reassuring hug.

"None that I can foresee. Although I will have to step in as an officer of the law once Jilly's parents have been told. I'll have to contact Alice Radford and advise her of the situation, too. As the social worker representing Children's Protective Services she's the one responsible for determining where Matthew will stay until the legal issues have been resolved. But there's no reason why I can't wait to alert Alice until tomorrow, too."

"Thanks, Jake...thanks so much," Megan murmured, leaning against his solid shoulder again.

He would have been well within his rights, not to mention following the letter of the law, if he had insisted on wrapping up the case that Saturday morning. But because of his consideration for everyone concerned, especially her, he chose, instead, to demonstrate just how compassionate he could be.

"It's no big deal," he said, giving her shoulder a squeeze.

"It is to me." Tipping her head back, she kissed him on the cheek. "You're a good man, Jake Cahill."

"Hey, I try to do the best I can with what I have," he tossed off lightly, then threaded his fingers through her hair, bent his head and kissed her on the mouth.

With a quiet sigh, Megan kissed him back, grateful beyond words that they had one more day together—

she and Jake and Matthew, who had begun to squirm in her arms.

"I think someone's ready for a fresh diaper," she advised, easing away from Jake.

"Perfect timing, as usual," he quipped in return, shooting her a rueful grin. "Want me to do the honors?"

"If you insist." Megan handed over the baby as they both stood. "I'll put on a pot of coffee and scramble some eggs and sausage."

"Then we can decide what we want to do with the rest of the day."

"How would you like to drive over to San Antonio? I've been wanting to freshen up the guest bedroom and the hall bathroom, and there's a new design store that's just opened there that specializes in the latest paint, wallpaper and fabric styles."

She wanted to stay as busy as possible doing something fun that day so she wouldn't have time to think about tomorrow and the eventual end result of all that would be set in motion then.

"Sounds good to me, as long as we have time for a stroll along the Riverwalk," Jake agreed.

"Maybe even an early dinner if Matthew cooperates," Megan added.

"Oh, he will," Jake assured her with more confidence than she had.

Considering it would be their first long road trip with the baby, Megan wasn't sure what to expect. Matthew was in good spirits, though, and the day turned out to be a success. He slept in his car seat on the drive to San Antonio, and seemed happy enough to ride around in his stroller, entertained by all the new sights and sounds.

Megan found exactly what she was looking for at the design store—sage-green paint for the bedroom, gauzy ivory fabric for the curtains, striped throw pillows in various shades of green and ivory to pile on the bed, and complementary wallpaper with tiny roses and sage-green vines on an ivory background for the hall bathroom. Then they took Matthew to the Riverwalk for a leisurely stroll followed by an early dinner.

Matthew began to fuss on the way to the lot where they'd parked Jake's car, but he dozed on the drive back to Serenity, lulled by the rhythmic motion as they rolled along the highway.

A wonderful day, Megan thought as she and Jake lingered over tucking the baby into his crib after giving him a last bottle. And a wonderful night ahead, she added to herself a while later when Jake took her by the hand and tugged her down the hallway to her bedroom. She needed no coaxing at all to shed her clothes and join him in her bed.

A week from now, her life would have changed all over again. Barring any major problems, Matthew would be reunited with his mother, and Jilly, in turn, would get all the help she needed from her parents. Jake, his duty done, would finally be able to consider taking the job Bobby Fuentes had offered him. On her own again, she would have time to finish her work on the history curriculum, when she wasn't busy painting, wallpapering or sewing curtains.

She should be relieved that she'd have nobody to worry about but herself. Once again, she could curl up in the emotionless cocoon she'd created for herself in Serenity, going about her business behind the cool and distant facade that had served her so well the past couple of years.

Only she didn't want to live that way anymore. She didn't want to trudge through dreary days or toss restlessly in the dark of lonely nights. Having opened her heart, her soul, to banished hopes and forgotten dreams—to Matthew and to Jake—she had become whole again. Without them, her world would fall apart unless she started, very soon, to accept what she couldn't change.

Tonight, though, she was going to open herself to Jake one last time. She was going to give herself up to his tender ministrations, and she was going to pretend, for one more night, that he would be there for her, always, as he had the past two weeks.

Shortly after noon on Sunday, Megan set aside the handset of her telephone and turned to face Jake. He sat at the kitchen table, hands wrapped around a mug of coffee, an expectant look on his face.

They had spent a lazy morning together, getting up early with Matthew, then going back to bed, although not to sleep, when the baby took his morning nap. Inevitably, though, the time had come for her to call Jilly.

While Megan showered and dressed in jeans and a sleeveless white shirt, Jake went back to his father's house to change into his uniform. When he returned to her house a short time later, Megan made the call.

"She's coming over?" Jake asked, meeting her gaze.

"She said she'd be here in half an hour," Megan replied, still standing by the counter, arms crossed over her chest. "She sounded surprised to hear from me, but she seemed eager enough to help out with Matthew. She said she can only stay until three, when she's expected home for Sunday dinner. I'm hoping that means her parents will be there as we'd hoped."

"More than likely, but we can track them down if we have to." Jake drank the last of his coffee, set his mug aside and stood slowly. "Guess I'd better be on my way." He hesitated, his reluctance to leave her obvious. "I'll head over to the station, contact Alice, and ask her to meet me there."

"I'll call you after we've talked to Jilly's parents so the two of you can join us at the Maitlands' house," Megan said, going over their plan one more time in a matter-of-fact tone, though she didn't feel the least bit businesslike about the confrontation that lay ahead.

She knew Jilly could react in almost any way once she was faced with the truth about her relationship to Matthew, but Megan had been fairly sure she could deal with whatever the young woman had to say. What if Jilly was in some sort of serious trouble, though? What if there had been something sinister about the way in which Matthew had been conceived, something Jilly desperately wanted to hide from her family?

What would she say to her then? Megan wondered. She had seen how much Jilly loved Matthew. So, quite naturally, she had also assumed the young woman must have cared for the baby's father, at least at one time. What if she was wrong and Jilly had something to fear from him?

"Are you sure you still want to talk to Jilly alone?" Jake asked, moving across the kitchen to stand in front of her.

Taking a deep breath, Megan nodded, then leaned against Jake's chest when he pulled her close for a reassuring hug.

"All right, then," he murmured, feathering a kiss on her brow. "You know where to find me."

Megan lingered in the kitchen while Jake let himself out the front door. She rinsed their coffee mugs, dried them and put them back in the cabinet, then checked to make sure she had a bottle ready for Matthew when he woke up from his nap.

She roamed around the living room, straightening cushions, and finally heard a faint whimper signaling that the baby was stirring just as she'd hoped. She had time to change his diaper, carry him downstairs and pop his bottle in the bottle warmer before the doorbell rang announcing Jilly's arrival.

"Perfect," she murmured, rubbing her cheek against Matthew's downy head as she went to answer the front door.

She wanted Jilly to be busy with the baby when she started asking questions—too busy to even think of running off.

"Hi, Jilly. Thanks for coming over," Megan said as she opened the door.

"No problem, Mrs. Cahill." Jilly flashed a slight

smile, then reached for Matthew. "Hey, big boy, how are you doing today?"

"He's ready for a bottle. Come out to the kitchen so we can talk while you feed him."

"Sure," Jilly agreed.

"Did your parents have a pleasant flight home yesterday?"

"Yes, they did." Jilly sat in one of the chairs by the kitchen table and took the bottle Megan held out to her.

"How was their trip?"

"They had a good time, I guess. We really didn't talk about it much. My father was more interested in my plans for the fall semester. He wants me to go back to Northwestern and he wants me to stay in premed, but I can't do that. I have...I have..." Her voice trailing away, she bent her head over Matthew.

Taking the opening she'd unexpectedly been offered, Megan continued.

"You have someone else to think about besides yourself now, don't you? Someone you love very much. Someone who needs you as much as you need him."

"What do you mean?" Jilly asked, her voice quavering as she met Megan's gaze.

"You're Matthew's mother, aren't you, Jilly?"

For several long moments, the young woman stared at her, a flurry of emotions fluttering across her lovely face—panic, at first, then denial, and finally acknowledgement edged with relief as she closed her eyes and nodded her head slowly.

"Oh, Jilly..." Megan moved across the kitchen to

stand beside her and put a comforting arm around her shoulders.

"How did you know?" Jilly asked in a faint voice.

"I didn't, at least not at first, and then, not for sure. I've suspected for several days, though. You were spending so much time here with him, and your feelings for him were becoming more and more obvious. I wanted to say something to you sooner, but I just couldn't believe that a young woman with all the advantages you've had would abandon her baby. Then, yesterday, Jake talked to the admissions clerk at the hospital where you gave birth. He agreed to let me talk to you before he gets involved."

"I'm going to be in a lot of trouble, aren't I?" Jilly met Megan's gaze again, desperation now underlying the fear in her eyes. "And I'm going to lose Matthew forever. But I can't. I just can't," she cried, tears filling her eyes. "I love him so much."

"Abandoning a baby the way you did *is* considered child endangerment, but you didn't put Matthew in serious jeopardy. You waited to make sure I'd found him before you left, and you've been looking out for his well-being, in your own way, the past couple of weeks."

"I would never do anything to hurt my baby. You have to believe me, Mrs. Cahill."

"I do, Jilly. But you did leave Matthew on my front porch, and for the life of me, I can't understand why. It was apparent that you took care of him until then, and you've just said how much you love him. So why abandon him? *Why,* Jilly?" Megan demanded angrily as she sat in one of the chairs facing the young woman.

"You're going to think I'm the silliest twit on the face of the earth, but I was afraid to tell my parents about him," she admitted, looking away in obvious embarrassment. "When I first found out that I was pregnant, I was sure they'd force me to have an abortion. Then, when it was too late for that, I was sure they'd make me give him up for adoption. So I decided to keep my pregnancy a secret.

"It wasn't hard, even when I was home for Christmas. I blamed my weight gain on the dorm food I'd been eating during the first semester, and I didn't see them at all after the holidays. Second semester, I talked them into letting me move into an apartment with a couple of friends, and they helped out after Matthew was born, even going to classes for me and taking notes so I could take my finals. I did pretty well, too, except for organic chemistry.

"I had intended all along to bring Matthew home for the summer. But my father was so upset when I told him I didn't want to return to Northwestern and continue in premed. I thought that if I could have a few weeks at home to sort of smooth the way, then I could tell them the real reason why I'd changed my plans for the future, and they would be able to accept Matthew into the family. But they were gone the first two weeks, and now..." She set the empty bottle on the table and shifted Matthew to her shoulder so she could burp him.

"Now they're going to find out that they have a grandson whether they're ready or not," Megan said.

"I left him here with you because I thought I'd be able to work up the courage to stand up to them if they tried to make me give him up. I can't do that, Mrs. Cahill. I can't give up my baby, and I won't."

Megan couldn't imagine how the Maitlands would receive their daughter's news. She hoped they would welcome the baby into their home, but she didn't want to give Jilly false hope. Edward and Diana Maitland had apparently had high expectations for their only child. They might not understand that Matthew was more important to her than anything, including a college degree.

"I don't think you'll have to do that, even if your parents won't help you," Megan assured her. "I, for one, believe you should be allowed to raise your child, and I'll help you any way I can."

"Oh, Mrs. Cahill, thank you...thank you so much." Jilly gazed at her, tears brimming in her eyes.

"What about Matthew's father?" she continued, determined to get as much information as she could. "Is he someone you cared for, someone you can include in your son's life?"

Looking away again, Jilly gave her head a negative shake.

"No. I mean..." she began, then drew a steadying breath. "I loved him very much. We met last summer while I was working at a camp in Minnesota, but he isn't really free to be a part of our lives. In fact, he doesn't even know about Matthew. I thought it was better not to tell him."

"But surely..."

"No, Mrs. Cahill, he doesn't need to know," Jilly

stated with such finality that Megan thought better of arguing with her any further, at least for the moment.

"Well, then, I suppose we'd better go to see your parents," she said, standing resolutely.

"Yes," Jilly agreed with a sigh of resignation. "We'd better..."

While she went upstairs to change Matthew's diaper, Megan called Jake at the police station.

"Give us about an hour, then head over to the Maitland house with Alice," she advised after relaying all that Jilly had told her.

"Are you sure you want to face them on your own? Especially since Jilly seems so concerned about how they'll react to her news."

"We'll be okay. Jilly's ready to tell them, and I think they'll take it better without too large an audience standing by. If they react too irrationally, I'll bring her and Matthew back to my house."

"See you in about an hour, then."

With Matthew secured in his car seat, Megan followed Jilly to her parents' house, parking behind the young woman's car in their driveway. Before going inside, Jilly took Matthew from her, hanging on to him for courage, Megan thought approvingly. The young woman had made some serious mistakes, but she was well on her way to righting them, and Megan intended to support her all the way.

They found Jilly's mother busy chopping vegetables in the large gourmet-style kitchen that was already filled with the aroma of roasting chicken. When Jilly, holding Matthew proudly in her arms, said that she had something to tell her parents, Diana Maitland hurried off to get her husband, who was closeted in his study.

As instructed, Megan and Jilly waited for them in the lavishly decorated formal living room, sitting side by side on the lush, floral-print sofa. Both of Jilly's parents wore the same slightly confused, slightly apprehensive expression on their faces when they finally joined them a few minutes later.

Megan was pleased with how simply and courageously Jilly told them about Matthew. Despite their obvious shock, and especially in her father's case, dismay, she stated the facts calmly, and included her reasons for abandoning the baby at Megan's house two weeks earlier. She also advised them that she intended to raise Matthew, on her own if necessary, as soon as she could prove to Children's Protective Services that she deserved to be given custody of him.

"But, darling, why didn't you come to us months ago?" Mrs. Maitland asked in a quiet voice.

Moving from the chair she'd taken earlier, she crouched in front of her daughter. Tentatively, she reached out to stroke Matthew's cheek with her fingertip, and Megan heaved a quiet sigh of relief. Diana Maitland seemed to have already begun to fall in love with her little grandson.

"I was afraid you would make me give him up for adoption so I could get on with my life the way you wanted me to," Jilly replied, her gaze fixed not on her mother, but her father.

He eyed her sternly for several moments, then, to Megan's even greater relief, his expression softened as he, too, rose to join Jilly's mother.

"We would never have forced you to give away our grandson," he said. "Not when you love him as much as we've always loved you. And you can still finish your college education. Lots of single mothers do, and you'll have us to help you, too."

"Oh, Daddy, thank you. And Mom, too. I'm so sorry I've caused so many problems. I never meant to hurt you, either. But I was so afraid…"

"We'll work things out, Jilly. I promise, we will," her mother vowed, taking Matthew and cuddling him close in her arms.

As happy as she was for Jilly and her parents, Megan felt a stab of pain deep in her heart. Their gain would be her loss very soon now, and though she had known the time would come eventually when she'd have to give up the baby, she wasn't prepared for the aching emptiness that had already begun to open up inside her.

The ringing of the doorbell announced the timely arrival of Jake and Alice Radford. Jake could have arrested Jilly and taken her to jail. But as chief of police, he chose to bend the rules and allow the young woman to remain in the custody of her parents until the following day when he had already arranged for her to go before a family court judge.

He advised the Maitlands to contact their lawyer, but also assured them, as did Alice Radford, that Jilly's youth and her obvious lack of malice toward Matthew would work in her favor. As for Matthew, Alice indicated that he would remain in Megan's care, at least until the following day.

Filled with mixed emotions, Megan opted to take

up Diane Maitland on her offer to stay for dinner so she and her husband could spend as much time getting to know their grandson as possible.

Jake didn't seem happy about the situation, but she assured him she would be fine. And when he offered to come over to her house later that evening, and she told him that she'd prefer to be alone, he seemed even more upset.

"I'm not sure that's such a good idea," he said as they stood together in the Maitlands' entryway.

"Please, Jake... I'll be fine," she insisted, willing him to understand. "I just need some time on my own tonight."

He gave in at last, albeit grudgingly.

"I'm taking you to the hearing tomorrow morning," he stated in a brook-no-argument tone. "It's scheduled for eleven o'clock. I'll pick you up at ten-thirty."

Taking her by the shoulders, he pulled her close and kissed her hard on the mouth.

"I'll be ready," she agreed when he finally turned to go.

Or at least she would try to be, Megan vowed as she joined the Maitlands in the kitchen where Matthew was now the center of attention. He belonged with his family, a family who was ready, willing and able to give him all the love he needed. She had done her job. She had kept him safe, and now it was time for her to give him up. No matter how much it made her heart ache.

Chapter Eighteen

As promised, Megan was waiting when Jake pulled up in front of her house on Monday morning. In fact, she was sitting on one of the rocking chairs on the porch with Matthew perched contentedly in her lap. Walking up the path, he saw that she had the car seat ready for him to secure in his car. She also had the stroller and diaper bag ready to go.

One would have thought that she was anxious to get the proceedings at the courthouse under way— proceedings that could transfer custody of the baby back to his mother, or more likely, to his grandparents. But the shadows under Megan's eyes and the thin, tight line of her mouth told another story altogether.

Had she slept at all the night before? Jake wondered, offering her what he hoped was a reassuring smile. Probably not, he decided. But then, neither had he. His concern for her had been too great. He'd had to stop himself several times from going to her house to check on her. In the end, only his fear of upsetting her further had kept him away.

"Hey, you and our little rookie cop didn't have to wait out here," he said as he climbed the porch steps.

"I like that—rookie cop." Trying with only limited success she returned his smile, then gestured toward the baby's things. "I thought it would be easier to have everything out here."

She shifted Matthew to her shoulder, stood slowly and smoothed a hand over her long, narrow black skirt as the baby gripped her pale yellow blouse in one tiny fist.

"There's no hurry." He grabbed the car seat with one hand, the stroller and diaper bag with the other, then added, "I don't think they'll start without us."

"No, I don't suppose they will," she agreed, the lightness in her voice sounding forced.

He wanted nothing more than to set aside the car seat and stroller so he could gather her into his arms. But he could tell by the set of her shoulders and the tilt of her chin that she was just barely hanging on to her composure. She wouldn't thank him if the emotions she had been working so hard to rein in broke free in a flood of uncontrollable tears.

With Matthew fastened into the car seat and Megan sitting beside him, staring silently out the window, Jake reached over and took her by the hand. Wordlessly, she clung to him, her grip tight, as he pulled away from the curb.

At the courthouse, Jake parked in one of the spaces reserved for police officers, then helped Megan settle Matthew in the stroller. Inside the old building, quiet on a small-town Monday morning in June, they saw Alice Radford waiting for them. Janet Humson of the district attorney's office, Diana and Edward Maitland, Jilly and Carl Wytze, a local and quite prominent attorney, were also seated on the benches lining the corridor.

Megan walked forward without the slightest show of hesitation, greeting everyone with a few words and a bright smile. Although Jake's heart ached for her, he was proud of how quickly she put the Maitlands and Jilly at ease.

"I was just telling Diana and Edward that Judge Richard Spalding has been assigned to the case," Alice advised as they all filed into one of the smaller courtrooms. "He's known to be very understanding and also very fair."

The judge, an old friend of Jake's father, joined them in the courtroom shortly and had his clerk call the hearing to order.

By one o'clock, he had been apprised of the situation in detail, hearing testimony about the baby's abandonment from Jake as the officer in charge of the case, Alice Radford as the Children's Protective Services representative, and Megan as the foster care provider.

All three of them had also spoken on Jilly's behalf. And Jilly, herself, very tearful and very contrite, had not only explained why she had left her son on Megan

Cahill's front porch, but had expressed, as well, her deep regret for behaving in such a foolhardy way.

Finally, Carl Wytze, Jilly's attorney, had asked for leniency toward his client. Ms. Humson, the district attorney, had agreed that under the circumstances, Ms. Maitland did not deserve the harshest punishment called for in child endangerment cases.

Just as Matthew—who had behaved like a perfect little gentleman, napping during most of the testimony—began to fuss, Judge Spalding called for a one-hour recess. After that, he indicated he would render his decision.

As they left the courtroom, Jake suggested that he and Megan take the baby to the café in the town square, where she could give the baby a bottle while they had a bite to eat. They talked very little, and then only about the court case and how the judge might rule. They agreed that although Judge Spalding had obviously disapproved of Jilly's actions, he seemed sympathetic enough to take into account her age and inexperience.

Megan also seemed to be in better spirits, which heartened Jake considerably. She had always believed that Matthew belonged with his mother, a mother she had insisted loved him. She was as prepared as she could possibly be to give up the baby if the judge ordered it that afternoon. And she would smile through it all, Jake knew. No matter how her heart might be breaking.

The reality wouldn't hit her until she was back home again, and all alone. Only she wasn't going to be all alone. Not if he had anything to say about it, and he intended to say a lot if she put up any protest.

To the satisfaction of all concerned, Judge Spalding ordered that Edward and Diana Maitland receive temporary custody of their grandson. After reprimanding Jilly severely, he then ordered her to take part in a parenting course offered by Children's Protective Services, and to perform two hundred hours of community service at the local women's shelter under Alice Radford's watchful eye. Following completion of the course and her community service, another hearing would be held to determine if custody of her son should be transferred to her.

A tearful, chastened Jilly thanked the judge, turned to hug each of her parents, then crossed the room to hug Megan, as well.

"Thank you, Mrs. Cahill. Thank you for everything," she murmured.

"You're welcome, Jilly." Megan stood back, hands on the young woman's shoulders, her gaze direct. "You have a wonderful son. Take good care of him."

"I will, I promise. And, Mrs. Cahill, I was wondering…Matthew hasn't been christened yet, and I thought maybe you might agree to be his godmother…."

"I'd be honored." Tears glistening in her eyes, Megan smiled as she hugged Jilly again.

"Chief Cahill, I'd like you to be his godfather, too," Jilly added, turning to him.

"I'd be honored, as well," Jake said, putting an arm around Megan.

"I'll let you know just as soon as we set the date."
Jilly beamed at them, then knelt down in front of
Matthew's stroller. "Ready to go home, baby boy?"
she cooed, tickling his cheek with a fingertip.

As the baby waved his arms and gurgled with
delight, Megan leaned against Jake. A soft, shuddering sigh rippled through her.

Glancing down, Jake saw that she was barely holding herself together. There was a crooked tilt to her
smile, a warning of how quickly it could slide away.
And the tears that had been only a glimmer in her
eyes moments ago now trickled, one and then another,
down her pale cheeks. Any minute she was going to
fall apart completely. And though she had every right
to, she would be angry with herself for spoiling what
she believed should be a happy time for Jilly and her
parents.

"Ready to go?" he asked softly, his grip on her
tightening as he feathered a kiss on her forehead.

Obviously not trusting herself to speak, she put her
arm around his waist and nodded.

It took longer than Jake liked to get Megan out of
the courthouse and into his car. Though she was just
barely hanging on despite the smiles she offered the
judge, Jilly and her parents, the lawyers and Alice
Radford, she wouldn't allow herself to be hurried
away until she had done what she considered to be
her duty to all involved.

Once they were alone in his car, however, she sat
back in the passenger seat, closed her eyes and sighed
deeply, unable to hide her exhaustion. Reaching over,
Jake took her hand in his, then started the engine.

"You did good in there today," he said.

"You, too," she murmured. Gripping his hand as if it were a lifeline, she turned to look at him as he pulled out of the parking lot. "I hope Edward and Diana realize how much you did for Jilly and for them. She could be on her way to jail instead of going home with her son."

"You did just as much for her as I did—more, in fact. Speaking up for her the way you did made all the difference to Judge Spalding."

"I only said what I believed to be true. Jilly might be immature, but she's never been malicious, especially where Matthew is concerned." She glanced out the window, then looked back at him, a frown creasing her forehead. "Where are we going?"

"Home."

"But my house is back that way." Megan gestured in the opposite direction.

"I know. We're going to my house, or rather, my father's house," Jake said.

He knew he was taking a risk. She was already feeling sad. He didn't want to make her mad, as well. But neither did he want her to be surrounded by reminders of Matthew's absence as she would be at her house.

"Why?" she asked, shooting him a quizzical glance.

"Change of scenery," he stated simply, giving her hand a reassuring squeeze. "I thought it might do you good tonight."

"Oh, really?" Her tone, to his relief, was more teasing than challenging.

"Yes, really. We can sit out by the pool for a while and have a glass of wine. Then I'll grill a steak and toss a salad. I even have dinner rolls to pop in the oven and an apple pie for dessert."

"Sounds...wonderful." Still clinging to his hand, she uttered a quiet sigh, then leaned her head back as he pulled into the long driveway leading back to the house tucked away from the road on an acre of manicured lawn.

They sat by the pool, and they shared a bottle of red wine. They never made it to the steak and salad, though. They shed their clothes and slipped into the pool as the sun dipped toward the far horizon. Then, naked, dripping wet, and giggling like naughty children, they scurried into the house and down the hallway to Jake's old bedroom where he still slept in the extra-long twin bed he had never bothered to replace.

They made love once in a frenzy of desire brought on by all the sexual teasing they'd done in the swimming pool, then again much more slowly, taking their time with deep, intimate kisses and the most tender of touches until neither of them could hold back any longer.

Afterward, Megan clung to Jake and cried softly. He held her and stroked her hair and spoke to her in hushed and soothing tones. Finally, she slept, curled trustingly close in his arms while he stared into the darkness, telling himself that the best was yet to be.

Thanks to Matthew, they had found their way back to each other. And while they couldn't change what had happened in the past, they could make the most of the future, together.

Chapter Nineteen

Megan awoke in the protective curve of Jake's arms, but she couldn't quite place where they were when she first opened her eyes. Gradually she remembered that he'd taken her to his father's house outside Serenity the previous afternoon. She also remembered why.

Lying close to Jake, savoring his warmth, she replayed the events of the previous day in her mind. Recalling the outcome of the court hearing at which Jilly's parents had been given custody of Matthew, she experienced again the odd mix of emotions that had almost overcome her then—joy for Jilly and her parents, sorrow for herself.

She had been too grateful to Jake for whisking her away from the courthouse to resist when he'd headed for his father's house. Nor had she resisted when he led her out to the chaise longue beside the swimming pool. Or when he teased her into shedding her clothes and going for a swim with him. And she had most definitely failed to resist when he led her into his bedroom, tumbled her onto his bed and made mad, passionate love to her.

Jake had come to her rescue last night just as he had so many times since she'd first found Matthew on her front porch. He had known exactly what she needed to help ease the ache of losing the baby she had grown to love as her own.

Though she hadn't really *lost* Matthew. By asking her to be his godmother, Jilly had guaranteed she would always be a part of his life. As Jake would be, too, as godfather.

But facing, on her own, the empty room she had used as a nursery the past two weeks was something Megan had dreaded. And Jake, bless his heart, had made sure she didn't have to. At least not when the baby's absence would have hit her the hardest.

Today she would have to pull herself together, though. She had leaned on Jake as long as she thought prudent. And she was much stronger now, more sure of herself in every way, than she had been that Friday morning when she'd stepped onto her porch to find an abandoned baby waiting for her there.

Caring for Matthew had helped her to make peace with the loss of her own child. And in so doing, she had also regained the sense of self-worth she had lost along with Will, and Jake.

She had finally made peace with Jake, as well, Megan thought, rubbing her cheek against the warm, bare skin of his chest. She could lie in bed with him, curled close enough to feel his heart beat, breathing in his masculine scent, forever.

Only that was the stuff of which fantasies were made.

In real life, *their* real lives, the time was drawing near when they would each have to go their separate ways again.

"Stop," Jake muttered, his voice a soft yet commanding growl that startled her out of her reverie.

"Stop what?" she asked, tipping her head back to meet his sleepy gaze.

"Stop thinking beyond this moment." He rolled on top of her with familiar ease, pinning her beneath him as he nuzzled her neck.

"I did more than enough of that last night."

"Oh, yeah?" He tugged at her earlobe with his teeth, making her shiver with anticipation. "I didn't know there was a limit on living for today."

"Eventually one must consider the future," she advised primly, even as she opened her legs to the gentle nudging of his knee.

"But surely with as much optimism as pessimism," he insisted, his deep voice edged with desire.

"I'm optimistic," she breathed, arching into his thrust. "But I'm also *realistic*."

"Megan, sweetheart, it doesn't get any more real than this...."

Afterward, when she was well and truly sated, though still not quite able to catch her breath, Jake slipped out of bed, pulling the lightweight cotton blanket over her.

"I'll make some coffee," he said, taking a pair of shorts from the dresser drawer. "Maybe rustle up some eggs. Are you hungry?"

"Famished," she admitted, pushing up on her elbows.

"Then I'll whip up some biscuits, too."

Her stomach growling a reminder that she hadn't eaten dinner the night before, Megan went to the closet, grabbed one of Jake's long-sleeved cotton shirts and put it on. Her clothes, as far as she remembered, were probably still strewn around the pool deck. She stopped in the bathroom to splash water on her face and make an attempt at combing the tangles out of her hair. Then, her stomach rumbling again, she headed for the sunny, spacious kitchen.

She hadn't quite reached the doorway when she heard the telephone ring.

Jake answered with a cheery hello, then added, "Hey, Bobby, what's going on?"

Aware that Jake's caller was more than likely his former boss, Special Agent in Charge Bobby Fuentes, Megan froze in the hallway. She also knew that she had no right to stand out of sight and eavesdrop on his conversation. But she couldn't seem to make herself continue into the kitchen.

"Oh, yeah? Sounds like you've got yourself a dicey situation," Jake continued after a few moments.

By the tone of his voice, Megan could tell he was interested in whatever Bobby had to say.

Another longer pause followed, then Jake spoke again, his words laced with what sounded like genuine regret.

"I wish I could help you, but I'm right where I want to be now."

Was he? Megan wondered. Was Jake really where he wanted to be? Or was he where he thought he had to be until he was sure he'd won back her trust?

"Thanks for thinking of me, Bobby. I appreciate the offer," Jake added. "But it's not something I want to do."

It could be a few months from now, though, as the same old small-town routine continues to grind away at you, Megan wanted to say. And would, she vowed as she walked into the kitchen.

"Coffee's ready," he said, smiling as he caught sight of her.

"I overheard your conversation with Bobby." She halted a few steps away from him, her gaze steady, her expression serious. "He wants you to go back to work for him, doesn't he?"

"He's broached the subject several times lately, but I'm not interested." Jake turned away from her to fill the mugs he'd set out on the counter.

"I can't believe that. You loved working undercover as a special agent for the bureau, and you were really good at your job. You've got to be bored to death here in Serenity."

"If I'm not mistaken, we talked about this once already." He carried the steaming mugs to the kitchen table and set them down. Then he crossed to where she stood, put one hand on her shoulder and tipped her face up with the other, forcing her to meet his gaze. "I like what I'm doing here just fine."

"For now, but what about a year from now?" she

demanded, shrugging away from him angrily. "I know why you came here, Jake—to mend our relationship. Now that we've done that, you don't have to stay any longer."

"Now that we've done that, Megan, there's nowhere on the face of the earth I'd rather be than here with you," Jake stated in a quiet voice. Moving to stand behind her, he put his hands on her shoulders and drew her back against his chest, then kissed her on the back of her neck. "I love you—always have, though there were times I didn't act like it. And I will always love you. You mean more to me than anything else."

Taking a step back, he turned her so that she faced him again. "I want to spend the rest of my life with you. I want us to be a family again—husband, wife and, God willing, a house full of children. And I want us to make a home together here in Serenity where I can do the kind of work I enjoy and still be a part of our family."

Megan couldn't discount the sincerity in Jake's voice any more than she could disallow the look of love in his vibrant eyes. They had gone through so much together, and then, so much too far apart. Against all odds, they were being given a second chance. All she had to do was trust him, as she once had, with her hopes and dreams.

She had vowed more times than she could count that she would never do that again. Could she take the risk now and follow her heart instead of her head? She loved Jake. Would trust follow?

"I want to believe you," she said, cradling his face

in her hands, the roughness of his beard bristling against her fingertips.

"Then do it, Megan. I won't let you down this time. I swear, I won't. You're more important to me than anything. You always have been. I just didn't realize it until it was almost too late. Unless it *is* too late...." His words trailed off as he searched her gaze, his bright eyes suddenly shadowed.

Faced with her moment of truth, Megan hesitated only a moment. She loved Jake and he loved her. Already they had so much more than most people. And loving him was a kind of trust in itself—the kind upon which a deeper, more complete confidence would surely grow.

"No, Jake, it's not too late," she assured him, giving him a quick kiss on the lips. "Not too late, at all. I never stopped loving you."

"Marry me, then—marry me again—Megan Cahill," he said, his gaze unwavering as he took both of her hands in his.

Drawing a deep breath, she clung to him, hesitating one last moment. Then, smiling at last, she nodded her head.

"Yes, Jake, I'll marry you—again."

With a whoop of joy, he pulled her into his arms, then planted a searing kiss on her lips. As she kissed him back with equal fervor, he shifted his hands from her shoulders to her hips, bringing their bodies into intimate alignment. She moaned low in her throat, arching into him in a not-so-subtle invitation.

"On the kitchen table or in the bedroom—your

choice,'' Jake muttered, breaking off their kiss as he lifted her into his arms.

Before she could voice her preference, they were interrupted by the ringing of the telephone.

''I'm not going to answer it,'' Jake growled, nibbling at her neck.

''You'd better,'' she said. ''You are the chief of police....''

''Ah, hell...''

Grudgingly, Jake set her on her feet, then lifted the receiver and barked a hello. An instant later, he eyed her quizzically as he spoke to the caller.

''Actually, I know right where she is. She's standing in my kitchen.'' He held the receiver out to her. ''Alice Radford,'' he said by way of explanation.

Her thoughts going immediately to Matthew, Megan took the receiver from Jake.

''Alice? Is something wrong? Is Matthew...?''

''As far as I know, Matthew is just fine. Unfortunately, I'm at the hospital with a three-year-old girl and her one-year-old brother, who aren't doing too well. Their mother died of a drug overdose about an hour ago, and I haven't had any luck finding next of kin. I need a foster home for them, pronto. I was hoping you could help me out.''

''What?'' Jake murmured, brushing a wisp of hair away from her face.

''Just a sec, Alice,'' she said, then repeated what the social worker had told her.

He listened patiently. Then, as if reading her mind, he nodded once when she'd finished. ''I'm willing if you are.''

Her heart bursting with love, Megan grinned at Jake as she spoke to Alice once again.

"Do you want us to come to you or do you want to bring the children to us?"

"I'll bring them to you. Just tell me where—your house or Jake's?"

"Mine," Megan replied without missing a beat. "I've still got the crib set up."

"I'll meet you there in about an hour. Unless you need more time…"

"An hour should be fine."

"Oh, I need to ask, as a Children's Protective Services rep, of course," Alice continued, a teasing note in her voice. "You two are going to make it legal, aren't you?"

"Oh, yes," Megan assured her. "We most certainly are."

"Are what?" Jake asked as she cradled the receiver.

"Going to make it legal," Megan said, stepping into his arms.

"Oh, yeah, just as soon as we can…."

Epilogue

Outside Megan's house that dark night in December, the weather was cold and damp, but inside it was warm and cozy as she helped Evie choose another ornament to hang on the Christmas tree Jake had just finished setting up in the living room.

The little girl, now almost four, shot Megan a sweet smile, then skipped over to Jake to show him the wooden Santa.

"See, Daddy? It's Santa Claus."

"I sure do, honey. Very nice," he said as he helped her loop the string over one of the lower branches.

Sitting next to Megan on the sofa, Evie's younger brother, Luke, who had just turned two a few days earlier, waved a plump, plush little snowman in the air.

"Mama…Mama…Mama…yook," he crowed. "Soman…"

"Yes, a snowman," she replied, tickling him under the chin.

"Here, let me give you a boost so you can put him high up on the tree," Jake said, scooping the little boy off the sofa and settling him onto his shoulders.

Luke giggled delightedly, clinging to Jake with one hand, the snowman clutched in the other.

As Evie climbed into her lap, Megan watched Jake help the little boy hang the ornament on the tree. Sometimes she couldn't quite believe just how happy she was.

She and Jake had been married at the end of July with Jake's father, Jilly and Matthew, Edward and Diana Maitland, Alice Radford and Margaret Griffin, along with well over a hundred other guests, in attendance. By then, Evie and Luke had already been a part of their lives for six weeks.

Now, six months later, the two children she and Jake had quickly grown to love as their own were about to become theirs by law. The final adoption proceedings were scheduled for the following week in Judge Spalding's court.

After the holidays, the four of them would be moving into Jake's father's house, now *their* house. They hadn't decided what to do with Megan's house yet, but there wasn't any rush. A few days ago, Megan had received a letter from one of her former foster sisters, saying she wanted to spend a few months in Serenity after the first of the year. Megan had offered her the house on Bay Leaf Lane as a temporary place to stay.

In mid March, right around the time Matthew

would celebrate his first birthday, Megan and Jake would be celebrating yet another special event of their own—the birth of their child.

"How are you doing, Mrs. Cahill?" Jake asked, sitting down beside her and tumbling Luke into his lap. "Not too tired, I hope."

"Not too tired at all." She leaned against him as he put one arm around her and splayed his free hand over her expanding tummy.

"Good, because I have plans for later."

"I like the sound of that."

"I was hoping you would."

Tipping her head back, Megan gave Jake a quick kiss on the cheek, then gave Evie and Luke one, too.

"Okay, let's see what else we have in here," she said, blinking back tears of joy as she turned back to the box of ornaments.

How blessed she was. More blessed than she had ever thought possible. And all because of the baby abandoned on her porch that not-too-distant day in June. Matthew had helped her open her heart again…to life and to love, to Jake and Evie and Luke, and to the baby growing inside her. She had everything she'd always wanted, and with Jake by her side, she trusted that she always would.

* * * * *

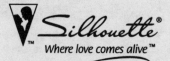

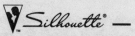

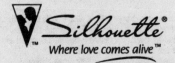